HUSH HUSH MURDERS

DEATH IN YACHT HAVEN

H R G WHITE

Other books by the author:
Hush Hush Murders Murder on the Road to Damascus
Order this book online at www.trafford.com
or email orders@trafford.com

Most Trafford titles are also available at major online book retailers.

Note for Librarians: A cataloguing record for this book is available from Library
and Archives Canada at www.collectionscanada.ca/amicus/index-e.html

Printed in Victoria, BC, Canada.

ISBN: 978-1-4269-2022-6 (sc)

ISBN: 978-1-4269-2023-3 (dj)

Library of Congress Control Number: 2009938985

*Our mission is to efficiently provide the world's finest, most comprehensive book
publishing service, enabling every author to experience success. To find out how to
publish your book, your way, and have it available worldwide, visit us online at www.
trafford.com*

Trafford rev. 1/25/2009

Trafford PUBLISHING® www.trafford.com

North America & international
toll-free: 1 888 232 4444 (USA & Canada)
phone: 250 383 6864 ♦ fax: 812 355 4082

To John and Hilda Gleason

CHAPTER 1

In a fraction of a second, the sun burst upon the watery horizon before Margaret realized the brightness of its light. Beyond her to the north she noticed the row of hollow masts with deliberately set loose lines. They slapped against the rows of masts in slips sculpted along the shore line as far as the marina boundaries reached toward the point of no return. These slips stretched out to form the marina's watery perimeter bordering the single torturous channel leading into that tiny inlet the locals since colonial times called Herring Bay. Just a moment before, it seemed all was at peace. The sound of the lines, once subdued, now became loud and raucous flapping ceaselessly in the wind gusts that suddenly swept across the Bay.

Out and away from the sights and sounds and glistening under the morning sun spread before them -- the serene wet -- the Chesapeake Bay. Flocks of Canada geese and Antarctic duck floated on the masked currents heading out to sea. It appeared that at certain fixed point, they would jump up off the water in unison. The flock would fly back up a mile or so, and then drop down to sit upon the south running current only to float back down the Bay.

Margaret chose that moment to jog along the pier only at Chester's insistence. Normally, she would have jogged past the entrance to the marina. Moments before the winter sunrise she noticed the pre dawn sky had been empty except for blue gray puff balls and the shell of a lacy moon. Those blue gray shadows splintered and then froze into sharp contrasts outlining the water smacking boats parked in their slips. Tide was high. Chop was light.

Moments before she was deep in thought over the matter of checking for frozen pipes and the water pump in the pump house under the kitchen. Her feet hit the white gravel path when Chester began to yip. He pranced ahead. He turned to bark and to posture in front of Margaret.

"What is it boy?" She knelt down to pet him. He whined, then puffed; then barked (really a yipping sound) then jumped away. His nostrils were wet. His breath turned to steam in the cold air.

Not yet winded, she got up to follow. The boat yard entrance to the marina loomed before her. The winding gravel road marked by the tiny Methodist chapel at its entrance from the highway was constructed over a silted in marsh. On either side of her, the grassy flat meadows glistened under the sun rising. Tufts of forgotten clumps of grass that had turned brown during the cold weather were now shriveled up under the boats resting upon travel and stationary lifts and jacks. Sail boats of assorted shape, size and state of disrepair resting on their sides appeared to sprawl scattered about the yard, but in reality were carefully placed so that if a storm were to come up and blow over a boat or two, the neighboring boat would not get a direct hit.

Some hulls were encrusted with barnacles. Most were not. They had already been scraped and cleaned before the onset of winter. On one or two; however, the main masts were broken off clean at the deck line. Here and there a skipjack was left as if abandoned among neatly stacked crab pots. These boxy motor boats were evidence of out of work watermen caused by the recent severe limitations the State wildlife commission set on last season's crab catch. Alarmed by the low yield of the highly prized rock, oyster and the crab catch, the State water commission issued drastic cutbacks in issuing licenses. The State's decision had taken its toll. The already diminishing fleet was in danger of disappearing off the face of the Bay.

Overwhelmed by the sudden appearance of a hanging corpse, Margaret knelt on the pier. The sight of the swollen blue head, projecting tongue, open lifeless eyes stunned her. It was swaying back and forth above the gentle moving ebb and flow. She heard only the sound of the clanking mast lines. The sight overpowered her senses. The thing that swung back and forth above her head was silent. It seemed as though the whole Bay was silent. She became ill and began retching over the side of the pier beyond the mooring cleats into an empty slip.

In sympathy Chester whimpered and tried to lick her face. She pushed him away. He gave up easily to sit on the cold wood planking growling and whining and yelping.

Above them pulling and tugging on a line strung to the yacht's mast, was a corpse. It was dressed in khakis and a wind breaker hung with its head resting grotesquely upon its chest. Shoeless, the corpse dangled on the line as limp as a rag doll, swaying slightly from the now sudden change to the mid winter tidal range that jostled and yanked at the Saber 28. The Saber was moored in the slip adjoining an Island Packet 38.

The silence was momentarily broken by a wind that caused the lines to slap against the main masts. The bobbing corpse hit the mast causing it to creak and groan under its weight.

She finally stopped choking and got up to catch her breath. She wiped her wet face with her packet of Kleenex stuffed in the sleeve of her sweat shirt. Dizzy she sat on the side of the pier for a long time looking up at the mast.

Chester jumped aboard the boat.

When he returned, Margaret got up to jog back up the dock to the gravel drive leading to the marina office. She tried to open the glass door normally open at this hour. She found it was locked; no sign of anyone inside. Everything was closed at that early hour in off season. The outside phone was out of order. The line to the receiver was cut.

Margaret was light headed and sick to her stomach.

They managed to jog a few paces and walk a few paces back to the house. No cars drove up along the road bordered on either side by deep ditches. The only sounds heard in the winds due East across the Bay were the popping sounds of hunters shooting at wary geese and ducks. Hunters dressed in green fatigues shot at game from behind floating camouflaged rafts.

The sound of the blood rushing in her head pounded in her ears.

"What is the matter with you girl?"

"Mr. Z. I just had a horrible experience. I've got to call the sheriff. Do you have a number?"

"Come in. Come in. I'll get it. I'll get it for you."

He took a piece of paper from the side of the refrigerator.

"Here it is. Do you want to use my phone? Here ya go. Take a cup of coffee," he took a mug out of the glass framed kitchen cabinet, put in some powered cream and filled with mug with coffee from a perculator.

"That would be good. Mr. Z."

Margaret dialed the rotary dial wall phone. No one answered at the sheriff's office. She left her phone number on the voice mail.

"No one answers. I left a message," she took a napkin from a napkin holder on top of a small kitchen table next to the door and wiped her face.

"County just cut back on services. I'm glad we still have trash pick up."

"How's the building business. Mr. Z?

"Bad part about making money is you gotta pay taxes."

"Yes. If you make money, you gotta pay taxes."

"I'm looking at redoing old buildings. Buying that old stuff and redoing it. And you know what? The other day they told me to drag down the price a little bit."

"To drag down the price?"

"On the resale. That dragging down the price cuts into the profits."

"Thanks. Mr. Z. I've got to get the dog back home. I'll let you know what has happened when I get a chance."

She ran across the yard, to her board walkway, up the steps and into the front room. Chester dropped a brown dock sider at the foot of Mr. Zadarius' steps and followed.

In a fit of peak she pulled off her sweatshirt, opened the phone book she found in desk drawer and began searching for phone numbers. This county's phone book was half the size of her home county's. She again called the nearest sheriff's office, then the mayor's office in the nearby township; then Edna May. On each attempt she had to leave a message on an answering machine. In the message she left with Edna May, she asked her to meet her at the house at the Point or to meet her at Irma's if she got down to the water before 9:30.

After replacing the telephone receiver, she sauntered into the kitchen to make a cup of coffee from water in the plastic jug. She brought several jugs from home. She gave Chester a bowl of water out of the tap, however. She then took a shower in the iron stained shower stall. The house water was from her well. She had a deep well.

Twenty minutes later the phone rang. It was the Sheriff. He asked her to come down to the marina to meet with him. They drove back. Chester elected to sit on his hind legs in the front seat. He whimpered and growled intermittently.

The recent winter ice storm left any of the young trees either split or snapped at mid trunk. They stuck up out of the wetlands brush like so many toothpicks. The accompanying ice flows on the Bay had all but disappeared despite the bitter cold. The morning was turning from blue white to gray.

Margaret parked the truck next to an abandoned skipjack. Chester jumped out of the truck behind her. They jogged to the dock beyond the boat ramp to find a county police officer nervously pacing back and forth.

"Good morning Ma'am."

"Hello officer I'm Margaret Longleaf. I'm down here looking over my aunt's property. She owns the old Allen place down in the Park."

He did not recognize the name or location.

"Did you call us?"

"Yes I did."

"Well Ma'am. We can't find any reported victim. In fact we can't find anything."

"I did see a corpse hanging from the mainmast on the Saber 28 over there," she pointed to the empty yacht.

"It's gone now," she added. She looked at her watch. "How long have you been here?"

"I got here about twenty minutes ago."

"It's been a good two hours since I called. Anything could have happened in the meantime. Let's go take a look at the boat."

"Who else saw this corpse?"

"Why Chester of course. Didn't you boy," she knelt down to pet the black lab. "In fact, if it wasn't for him, I would not have come out onto the dock at all this morning."

"What time was that?"

"About six thirty or so."

"Sunrise?"

"Yes. Or just before sunrise. The sun comes up late this time of year."

"And what did you see," he asked with some impatience. He was young, fair complected; a university type.

Margaret did not rush to answer.

"After Chester led me to about this spot and stopped, I looked up at the row of masts. I was really looking for a blue heron or osprey. Sometimes they winter over. I thought Chester had spotted a bird. I saw something swaying back and forth. At first I thought it was a blue heron."

"Why?"

"Why? I don't know. The color I think. I remember that I was afraid it had gotten caught up in the mast lines.

"As we got closer, the sun came up and I could see it better. It was a corpse all right. Its head hung down on its chest. It looked more like a woman than a man. He had on gray-blue trousers. He was not very big in size if you catch the drift."

"Are you sure you saw a person?"

"Hanging from that mast?" She carefully stepped to mid ship to point to the mast.

"Oh yes, quite sure. Look for yourself. You can still see the loose lines. It looks as though they've been cut."

The officer made a few more notes, picked up his radio microphone and called in some information. After a few minutes he returned.

Chester, in the meantime, stood in a cloud of steam of his own making. He had become increasingly agitated. He began to pace back and forth up and down the dock that stretched the full length of the boat slip.

After several minutes the officer returned.

"Are you OK ma'am? I'm sorry there's nothing we can do but take a complete report."

"Yes. You should do some sort of a search. There is something wrong here. Something very wrong."

"What makes you say that?"

"Look at Chester. He's agitated. I suspect that the victim is still around here somewhere."

"I'm sorry, but our hands are tied. We'd have to get a search warrant."

"I suggest you get one," a tear streamed down her face.

He walked away to talk on the car phone.

"Can't do that ma'am. I've been instructed to leave the boatyard. You're going to have to leave also."

"Trespassing?"

"Yes."

"I think whoever gave that order is a little out of line."

"Why do you say that?"

"We rent a slip here in this boatyard. We do have access rights. Can we talk further after I've gotten some breakfast at the Inlet?" Margaret noticed that she had forgotten to tie her right show lace. She knelt down to tie it.

"Yes ma'am. If you'd come by the office this morning."

"Sure. I should pay a call to the Mayor."

"Mayor's gone to Pompano for the month."

"Oh dear. Then in the meantime can you meet me at Irma's?"

* * *

Breakfast was served in a room that was built as an afterthought. It was built on the pier behind the ramshackle building facing onto the road to the Deale Bridge. On roadside two small windows allowed only a bit of light into the anteroom. Margaret walked through the dank bar. Cigarette smoke from the evening before still filled the room giving everything a hazy look. Despite the early hour, a bartender and one patron sitting at the circular bar were deep in conversation over a small round glass of Coors light. Thick paper coasters littered the bar top. The juke boxes were lit, but not playing. The room seemed dank in the gloom.

"Good morning," Margaret said in passing not wanting to appear snotty. She got a nod from the bartender.

Strips of plastic hung from the door between the bar and the restaurant. Patches of light moved continually across ceiling from the glare of the morning sunlight mirrored off the surface of the fast running creek. The slap of high tide against the bulkhead jostled the room ever so slightly.

Margaret picked one of the Formica tables in the center quadrant window so that she could look out over the creek and admire the huge Victorian sideboard at the same time. This piece of furniture sat next another, but it was topped with an ornate hutch lining the wall backing up to the bar and to the passageway to the kitchen. Behind her at a table in the corner sat two men who talked at length. She listened carefully while waiting for the waitress to take her order of coffee and toast before scurrying to the cook to carry the order to prepare creamed chip beef, pancakes, scrapple, and grits. She appeared once to pour juice and coffee for Margaret and for the men seated behind her.

On an impulse, Margaret got up to pick up a copy of the morning Post from the buffet stopping only to admire the chocolate and lemon frosted cakes, peach, apple and blueberry pies displayed in glass covers on various levels of the hutch. As she returned to the table she casually glanced at the two men in the corner. They were wearing worsted wool and suede jackets, talking loudly and in a cavalier manner.

When Margaret met Edna sometime later, she recounted not only the missing corpse episode, but also the strange conversation. Of the two unrelated incidents, Edna was more interested in the conversation.

"I tell you that Daniel is not at all interested in proposition one eighty four. Miss Oh Miss. Could you bring us some cream?"

"Well, I can tell you he is going to be sent out to RISMAR Headquarters to manage the project at least until the whole situation calms down. He's supposed to see the doctor about his kidney stones this morning.

Then he catches the afternoon plane on Friday. He should arrive Monday morning."

"He's going out to replace Guy. Guy was sent down." He paused for a moment. "As they say. You don't think George wants to take that tour do you?"

"Certainly not. The old poison tour. But someone has got to step in until a new director is selected. Bye the by." He lowered his voice, "Guy is already back here. He showed up at last night's staff meeting. Fit to be tied."

"For a RISMAR director, he was relieved pretty quick. I hate black coffee. Where is the waitress?"

They moved their chairs.

"What does that tell you. He can kiss his career goodbye. He was probably out there too long. By the way where is that waitress?"

"No telling," the dark haired man dressed in a dark suede sports jacket and tie chuckled. "What went on at post anyway?"

"Well George that's a matter of opinion. Let me give you a scenario. We've got four support centers in addition to the central staff at RISMAR."

"Yeah."

"Guy was questioning why the support for all of the systems are handled separately. He thought that because Finsoft was already processing data in the mainframe at RISMAR over the wide area network with central staff messaging the data anyway, he could centralize the processing."

"What is Finsoft?"

"Financial software George."

"What did the four support centers do anyway?"

"The satellite support centers as they are called handled all of the problems the local users reported. It's that simple George."

"Were they different? Sounds like they were parallel. Local users at each site could just have the same kind of problems."

"Yes. The sites were configured the same."

"Running in parallel has its advantages. Especially if there is a natural disaster at one of the sites."

"Listen to me. Guy is concerned with saving money on salaries only. He doesn't care about the sites. He claimed that by consolidating these sites and beefing up security, he could save the company as much as a million dollars in salaries and benefits over a three year period."

"I think that is overestimating. In fact, I think I just made an understatement. Did he have any facts to back this up?"

After a pause, "I don't think so. Just canceling the contracts on the equipment would add up to a million dollars in additional costs. I bet he figured in maintenance personnel costs too. As part of proposed savings to the company."

"Now George. That's popular talk these days. Getting rid of high tech personnel is in right now. No thinking corporation wants to carry a bunch of retirees on the books."

"Only very expensive retired execs."

They both laughed.

"But as a practical matter. Let's look at what would happen if a monsoon destroyed the center or even a satellite dish. RISMAR would be down for hours or even days. Some of our mission critical functions would be severely impacted."

"Look here ole buddy," he stopped for a moment. "All of this stuff about mission critical functions that are run in real time. We do nothing in real time. What is with a high level of reliability or performance or even security." He stopped and lowered his voice.

"We've never worked in that kind of environment. What gets done -- gets done because it's the politically correct thing to do.

"He'll tell you himself."

"Who George? Who will admit it?"

"Guy himself. He should have been here an hour ago. He's found a new and cheaper contractor. The bid came in from London. Somebody is supposed to show tonight." He drummed his fingers on the table.

"Excuse me Mrs. Longleaf. Do you mind?"

Margaret looked up from the Metro section of the paper to find Sheriff McNearny seating himself across from her. She had not yet been served her breakfast.

"I hope you don't' mind." He could see her hands were shaking. He didn't speak to her for a long time.

At that moment the waitress reappeared with Margaret's pancakes, coffee and juice and the order for the men behind her - one order of creamed chip beef and one of pancakes, scrapple and grits. When she returned, Margaret noticed she wore an apron with Alma stitched on it. She poured a cup for the young officer. This task began her hovering activities. She never strayed very far from their table. If she went into the kitchen almost immediately, she would reappear with something for the Sheriff. She brought extra napkins or clean flatware or extra butter and cream.

The two men sitting behind Margaret took advantage of Alma's sudden appearances, and spent their time asking her for more coffee, juice, cream, and butter, napkins while plying her with questions about the weather, road conditions, and the size of the chop. Complying with the string of requests or answering questions did not seem to dampen her curiosity. She stayed within earshot.

Beyond them in the southeast corner of the cafe a group of heavily clothed watermen sat at Formica tables. These tables neatly lining the south end of the restaurant overlooking the swift running creek. They were dressed in plaid shirts or polo knits, long sleeved. Their slickers were hung on brass hooks nailed to the nearby kitchen wall facing west. They talked incessantly as if in competition for attention from the swells. They gradually became subdued under smoke rings. After a while the whole restaurant became silent. he morning sun again broke through the cloud mass.

CHAPTER 2

Edna opened her briefcase on her lap. She took out a sheaf of papers and set them on the table.

"Here take this," she handed Margaret a legal pad.

"I've put together a list of repairs and I've ranked them in order. All you have to do is get some estimates on how much each will cost."

"I can't do this."

"Why?"

"I'm upset."

"Oh. Why yes of course. Of course, you are. I've called Tory. In fact, I called him just after I talked to you. He is on his way. He's bringing his boat. It will take a day to get here. He will be cruising up the bay."

"Tory?"

"You've met Tory Wayles. Tory is just a nick name."

"Yes. Of course. It's been a couple of years. So he's coming by water."

"In deed. That way he can inspect the dock. Say look at this cup. It's cracked."

***

"I don't think we're approaching this logically," Edna said.

"What?"

"Look Margaret. This beautiful pressed glass," with that she pulled open the hand blown glass door to a country corner cupboard. The hinge was loose. She pushed a small brass screw back into place, took out a goblet and held it up to the light flickering from a converted ship's berthing lamp.

Outside the cold winter dusk was all that was left of another overcast wintry day. The dusky rose colored sunset of oranges and pinks had dimmed the sky light so that the only other lights on the street were those across the road in the laundromat. On this particular evening no one was in the laundromat except for Donna. She stood at the large bay window peering across into the antique shop. It was mid winter.

Behind them in the back of the shop an old Seth Thomas chimed. It held a tinny sound. The last chime stopped abruptly thus disrupting the rhythm.

"We've got to rethink our approach to this puzzle," she repeated in a hoarse whisper.
"In what way?"

"Well let's see. What can we possibly do," she picked up another goblet to examine it. "Late nineteenth century wouldn't you say? Pre world war one anyway."

She put it down and then proceeded to carefully examine each one that lined the shelf. Each was pressed in a different pattern.

"We've got a missing corpse."

"We've got a missing corpse and a missing Saber," Margaret corrected.

"You mean the slip was empty?"

"Yep. I drove back to check. It's as empty as a bay harbor in a hurricane."

"Not even any oil trailings?"

"Don't remember seeing any. Why?"

"Then. Then it might still be in the marina."

"But where? Besides it has a tiny engine. It might not have left any oil trailings."

"The water is very milky this time of year. Even the tiniest of tracings are leaked especially coming in and out of the marina. They've got to use an engine. Unless it was pulled out by another boat."

"I don't like that theory Edna. Another boat would have left oil trailings."

"Either the boat left that slip in the marina under its own power or it was towed by another boat. Or. Listen to this theory. It was towed by hand."

"Hello. Hello there."

"Hi Danny," Margaret turned and greeted the shop owner as he approached.

"Well darlings," he kissed Margaret and Edna May. "What brings you down this way?"

"I came down to check on the house."

"Do you have any Meissen?" Edna interrupted. She sheepishly put the pressed glass goblet back into the cupboard, shut the door, and wiped one of the bulging glass panes with the edge of her hand.

"Let's take a look. Follow me."

She followed him toward the southeast end of the shop through a maze of Victorian sideboards of cherry, pie safes of oak and punched tin, dressers of walnut with carved acorn drawer pulls to a small office hidden behind a china closet placed in an awkward position that required some thought to safely maneuver around it. A small electric heater was placed in the center of the room upon the bare cement floor. Its heating elements glowed red in the gloomy, windowless room. Periodically, the elements gave off a cracking sound.

"Eddie where is your significant other?" he turned and held her hands.

"He's no longer with the Secretary. He retired some time ago. After thirty-two years, not even a by your leave. Now all he does is sit in his room and listen to the radio. In the spring he'll go out and work in the garden with Seth of course. That is unless he gets a consulting contract, but just now they're pretty infrequent," her voice trailed off.

"No. I don't mean him. The one who owns that sleek little French boat. He parks in the marina near Pax creek."

"Tory?" She paused. "Around I suppose. We haven't used his services lately." And under her breath, "But I think we will be using them in the very near future."

"Just out of curiosity what are his services my dear?"

"Tory? He's an independent contractor."

"I thought he was just another marine engineer loitering around the dock," he threw his head back and laughed.

"He works on engines. His own mostly. He does some investigating too. For insurance companies. Recently marine insurance fraud. Are you parked down there too?"

"No. I'm not a vet. I used to see him up here at Blake's marina."

"You've got a boat?"

"Used to have a slip."

"Just out of curiosity how is the turnover at Blakes?"

"If you mean how many times or I should say, how often boat owners transfer in and out of the marina. It's a very low turnover rate, because the rents are the cheapest south of Annapolis."

"Power or sail?"

"We're purists. We were. We're strictly sail. Or I should say were strictly sail," he sighed.

"So you were moored on the sailing side of the marina. Margie which slip are you interested in?"

Margaret was in the midst of studying the condition of the wooden weights of a cherry grandfather's clock. The clock was keeping perfect time. It was crafted in western Maryland with the name of the town hand painted in gold and black at the top of its face. A typed written letter was taped inside the cabinet just behind the pendulum. This document was to serve as a source of authentication and of its history. The author was careful to list the important dates beginning with the date of creation 1789. The name of the clockmaker, Karl Messerschmidt, was the only information given on the artisan. Nothing, not even his age at the date the clock was crafted. The text of the document had the pica shape and was most likely typed on an old Olivetti. It began with, "Let it be known to all ye present the bearer of this instrument possesses true ownership of this Messerschmidt clock crafted during the great revolution, years of great hardship." Because of the dim lights, she could not read the entire document.

"Sixteen or seventeen. The one up near the cart shed," Margaret called from that corner of the shop now dark except for the single hanging Tiffany lamp.

"I'll be right back. I'm going out to the truck to get a flashlight." The bell over the door jingled. She waved to Donna. Donna waved and turned.

"That's on the sailing side all right," he confirmed.   "I   think   I've got an old association slip diagram somewhere in my files," he began rifling through an old glass enclosed bookcase. After several minutes of methodically searching the tiers of shelves, he pulled out and handed Edna a folder marked Dockers Association. Shadows covered the top and left side of his face.

"I'm presuming that you're interested in nineteenth century," he leaned from a train station master's chair to turn up the light intensity of the lamp under a green glass shade. The pine chair once used by a train station master squeaked.

"What? Oh, yes. Say can I borrow this folder?"

"And do you want castle scenes?"

"Got any ruins?"

"What? Are you talking about my life?"

Edna became silent as if waiting for the next admission.

"Well my life is in complete shambles at this point," he sighed again. He pulled out an old wooden box filled with lined three by five cards. He had them sorted out by category using alphabetized index cards. He began with the letter c for china. He then went to m for Meissen.

"Life and times," Edna mused. She was concentrating on reading the covenants of the Dockers Association in the dimness and not really listening.

"We had a really great thing going. I even left my very demanding job on the House Finance Committee. I'd been on that job for ten years."

"Those jobs are prestigious all right," Edna interrupted gently with one of her famous understatements.

"I left that job to open up this little out-of-way place. I poured everything I had into this little project. My heart and soul if you know what I mean," he spoke over her words. He spoke not looking at Edna, but as though he were speaking a monologue of thoughts that needed to be spoken.

"It takes a certain amount of commitment."

"Seven days a week. And what do I have to show for it? I may just well lose this place. Where will I go? What will I do?"

"Danny. Wait a minute. What's happened?"

"We've split up," he spoke quietly.

"I wondered why I hadn't seen Max lately. When did this happen?" Edna crossed her leg and leaned forward.

"It's been six months anyway. Just moved out without a word. Left a pile of his bills. And started a court action on top of that."

"Sounds like a property settlement to me."

"Would you give me some advice? I don't know how I can pay you right away. I practically broke."

"OK I'll charge you a cheap rate provided we do a swap."

"What is cheap?"

"Fifty dollars an hour."

"Swap? What kind of swap?"

"Information swap only," she shrugged. "And maybe some discounts on antique stuff."

"I don't know. I just don't know," he sighed again. "It depends."

He sat almost slumped under a stream of light filtering down from the old train station lamp. Shadows dark purple in color covered areas of his face that appeared to be hollowed out around the eyes, sunken under the cheek bones and in the hollows of his temples. Edna reached out and held his hand for a moment.

He was cold to the touch.

"Danny. I know that you won't be able to accept this for a while. But things will get better. When one door shuts on you, another opens."

"What did you say?"

"Danny. Sell your house. What do you need a house for anyway? Use that money to buy out your partner. Move into the store. Look at this room. You can fix it up."

"What?"

"Put your house up for sale today."

"What? How can I?"

"How can you not?"

"Suppose Max comes back?"

"But suppose Max does not come back."

"Do you know something that I don't know Edna?"

"No. Don I don't know anything about this situation you've gotten yourself into. But I can tell you this I have a very bad feeling about it. Something is not right. Max is a very responsible person. Something is very wrong. But whatever has happened, you have got to prepare yourself for the worst. Do you carry any kind of partnership insurance?"

"OK. OK," he took off his wire rimmed glasses and threw them on the top of the desk. "You know it all started about a year ago. Longer ago maybe now that I think about it. I feel so devastated. Betrayed is the word. I couldn't talk about it at first. I decided that I must have done something terribly wrong. Somehow, sometime, some place I decided I must have done something so awful that I deserved this of inhumane treatment. I know I'm making excuses, but lately I have come to realize that the whole thing was planned."

"In what way?"

"But then something happened. Whatever it was that was going on stopped. It stopped suddenly," he ignored her question.

"What stopped suddenly."

"Stressful confrontations for one thing. Strange phone calls in the middle of the night for another. For the first time in a long time, I'm getting a full night's sleep."

"At least I think it's slip fifteen," Margaret came into the room. She spoke above them in the darkness. She had taken off her lined Burberry raincoat. It was draped over her left arm. Her black and white tweed cotton socks, black and white plaid slacks, and black turtle neck sweater were barely visible in the dimness.

"Not only that, but the bills have not been paid."

"That reminds me," interrupted Margaret. "I haven't paid my bills. I have got to get back. I'm going back in the morning that is unless you have any objections Edna."

"It's what is so strange about this whole situation. Max always paid bills on time. Was so conscientious about everything. He may have purchased partnership insurance. I must call the accountant."

"I really didn't know Max that well, but he certainly seemed level headed to me. He certainly was a successful business man," Edna interrupted.

"For a while I'd get notices of unpaid bills. I couldn't even verify that they were actual expenses. Then all of a sudden; those long unexplained absences became one long continuous one. Would argue at the drop of a hat and for no apparent reason."

"Danny. That sounds like Edna on her best days." Margaret interrupted his thought stream. She stood in the doorway. The glass door to the shop rattled behind her as winds buffeted against the building. The shade, half drawn, slapped against the glass encased door frame. She spotted the open folder that lay in Edna's lap. She picked it up and used her flashlight to examine the slip diagram. After scanning the diagram, she pulled out a pencil from her purse and marked the slip in the diagram with the letter x. After she pulled out one of the attachments, she put the folder back on Edna's lap. With her finger, she pointed to the slip that was marked with an identifying number beside the penciled x mark. Under the light of the flashlight which she held under her arm, she turned the pages to those filled with names and addresses beside the matching slip numbers.

"Margaret dear that's why I went into law."

"What?" he asked absentmindedly.

"Danny. Don't pay any attention to this silly conversation," Edna turned her attention back to the marina covenants.

As if on cue, Margaret abruptly left the room. She switched off the light, put the attachment in her purse, then switched on her search light as soon as she left the office. Its light could be seen sweeping the dimly lit shop outside the office doorway.

"Margaret what are you looking for?" he called. "It looks like a lighthouse out there," he said to Edna in a low voice.

"Maybe I can help you."

"I'm not looking for anything in particular," she went back to reading the type written text on the sheet of parchment scotch taped to the inside of the grandfather's clock.

And in from the consuming darkness, sounds of north easterly winds sweeping down the expanse of the bay seemed to pick up momentum at this location, its widest point and began to howl buffeting more frequently now against the nondescript two story building. The lights flickered on those occasions when the momentum of the winds became so fierce that they overpowered the lines strung up and down the wet lands road leading to the marina.

"What? I don't think our conversation was in the least silly," he appeared bewildered. He pulled the cuff of his sweater over the sleeve of his hunter green and navy blue plaid shirt. He wore kaki pants year round.

"Let me ask you this," Edna ignored his observation. "When was the last time you took out the boat?"

"That's ancient history."

"Tell me approximately. Was it last spring? Maybe just after repairs to the bilge pump," she was guessing.

"No. No. A little more recent" he didn't seem to notice that Edna was guessing. He tapped his fingers on the desk. He stood up to face the train station clock encased in tiger maple. Its upper face was partially hidden in the shadows. He went over to it to open the painted glass door. He adjusted one of the weights then the other. In the process he knocked the pendulum. He stopped its movement. Then with great care he adjusted the pendulum's point and gently pushed it to start its motion again. He closed the case door and turned the handle to lock it.

"I'd have to say late October or maybe early November. Weather was gorgeous on that particular day. Warm. Plenty of wind. Light chop. No clouds. We actually sailed in one of the regattas. Came in third as I recall. I won that wind breaker," he pointed to a green and red nylon jacket hanging on a clothes tree at the left hand side of the door.

"She was fine little sailer Her deck and trim were teak. Built in Nicaragua. One of the infamous Nicaragua brothers had her built. She was sleek not gaudy even though she had an oddly shaped fore and aft and an elongated cockpit very oddly placed. She was built to race probably as a gun runner. The story goes that she was bought by a millionaire out of Miami. He brought her up to Florida. And in the course of human events went broke. That's when Max spotted her," he returned to his chair to resume his search within the confines of the wooden index card box.

"Here we are," he pulled out an index card. "I've got a soup tureen. Somewhere here in the shop. Now where did I put it."

"And that's the last time I was out on the boat," he turned the swivel chair toward the sound of a loud clatter.

"Is everything all right?" he called out.

They both got up.

CHAPTER 3

"Hey. Someone is in the marina office. Let's go in."

With that observation, Edna decided to pull her car into the marina office complex and carelessly parked her car in the gravel drive. Bits of gravel were thrown up into the tire wells making a racket as the tires crunched into the blanket of gravel covering the perimeter of the parking lot. When Edna turned off the car lights, the outside darkness was suddenly pierced by starlight. Lights from powdery streams of star packed constellations appeared to flicker as a gauzy canopy of grayish clouds moved across the moon. These ephemeral dots of light stuck up behind the moon gave the impression that they were strewn across the sky in great clumps. And below them were the howling winds. Thundering down upon the bayscape came flesh knawing winds that burst about in packs of annoying gusts fiercely cold and wet. Lines slapped incessantly against the rows of masts bouncing up and down on the rough incoming tide.

The engine spun out with a single grind then silence.

"Did anyone ever tell you that your car looks like and even acts like a green beetle."

"My Buick. A rhinoceros beetle. I think beetles are gray not green," Edna could not resist correcting. "She lumbers along all right, but she's reliable enough. With an old car, you've got to do a lot of maintenance. I'm always checking the oil. I put a quart in her once a month. Or I should say a quart or two."

"Did you say you saw someone in the office?" asked Margaret as they walked around the east end of the building to dockside. "I don't see any lights."

The building, a rectangular two story with a New Orleans French Quarter porch on the second story, was constructed of cinderblock and painted yellow ochre. It sat on the dividing line between the motor powered boats and the sail boats.

They found an interior light on behind the harbor master door. Edna attempted to open the door. It was locked. She then knocked. After some minutes, a young woman appeared and unlocked the door. It became more and more apparent that she was waiting for someone. And as the conversation progressed they made half hearted attempts to correct the impression at those instances when she mistook them for her expected visitors.

"Hi. I'm Edna Keach and this is Margaret Longleaf. I've got a question for you," before waiting for a response she added. "What is the story behind this color?" She slapped the building facade.

"Well hello yourself. I'm Willa Thompson. The answer to your query is quite simple in concept. The color was painted on this building so as not to confuse the boat owners. You'll notice the color of the restaurant next door is pink," she said this in a matter-of-fact tone of voice. Her accent sounded as though she was raised on Smith Island.

"Color coding. Of course. That's too subtle for me. It's like the color coded chart identifying the classes of boat owners."

"Yes," she turned toward Edna for a moment. "The white dots are for sail and blue ones are for motor."

"I've noticed that the sail boats are closest to the channel."

"Not all. Some are at the back of the marina near the wetlands."

While Margaret was talking with the young woman, Edna closely examined the marina diagram pinned to the south wall. She wrote notes on a piece of paper that she retrieved from her shoulder strap purse.

"We've come to ask for some technical advice," Margaret ad-libbed.

"That I've got quite a bit to offer. No matter the subject," she smiled.

"Say. Do you know you've got the Mary Darling anchored here?"

They ignored Edna's clucking.

"It's about renaming an old boat that I am thinking about buying from a friend. You know," she paused for several long seconds, "without attracting bad luck."

"Oh of course. Of course. You can do several things. But before you do anything get her cleaned up. Be sure you sand off her old name, then prime and paint her all over a different color. Say an antique white versus a brilliant white. Something very subtle."

"OK. OK. That's the first step."

"Yep," she adjusted her wire rim glasses on the bridge of her nose.

"Then at the point when you decide to rename her, you've got to be very careful how you go about this," she sat down at her desk behind the counter and began to look through a stack of papers.

"If possible rename her using the same name only in another language Italian or Greek maybe," she said over her papers.

"What else?"

"Well if she's named for a woman and you don't like the name, rename her for the shipbuilder's daughter or mother."

"Why?"

"It shows that you want to continue the connection with the previous good luck spell that the boat is under and that you want this good luck to continue. Or better yet. Now try this one on for size. Have the boat owner that you're buying the boat from change her name before the title actually passes to you."

"Wow," Margaret smacked her lips. "Seriously."

"And don't forget the christening ceremony. It is during this ceremony that you officially ask the gods of wind, rain, and sea to permit you continued good fortune. In addition to all of these precautions, Father Hazlit has a special blessing of the fleet down at the inner city dock in the early spring."

"Across from the market?"

"Down further the quay. Across from the Quail and Hound."

"Do you know anything about the Sea Quark?"

"Which slip."

"Seventeen. It's two slips down on the left. She's at the end."

"Describe her."

"A Saber. New. We can't find her."

"Don't know that one."

"Say. Aren't you from St. Michael's?" Edna popped up.

"I'm from Cambridge. Been here since last summer. Came over from Wicomico Creek. That's a very nice marina. Say wait a minute. The Sea Quark is still about."

"What does the S stand for?" Edna pointed to the grid at the top of the chart.

"Scunner class."

"You're kidding," Edna commented without turning around. She continued to study the diagram.

"Yeah. I'm kidding," she rolled her eyes.

"Say can we go out to take a look at her? Do you know how long she's been parked here?"

"Sure. You'll find her in the usual place, but not for long. I'll have the contract ready when you get back."

"Oh. We're not here for that contract," Edna called back simultaneously shutting the door and pushing Margaret out onto the dock.

Her response was lost in the fog drift.

"What happened to the clear sky? How long were we in that office?"

They looked out upon the mist enshrouded marina. The air was so thick with moisture that they could not see to the end of the pier directly in front of the harbor master's office.

"Too long. Much too long Margaret. Ever seen such a fog. This is a stealth fog. Come on follow me."

"Just who is Edna Keach? Certainly not you."

"What? Oh that. Margaret I thought you knew. It's just a play on words."

"We're heading away from slip seventeen."

"I want to see another ship. She's got an odd name."

The planks on the circumferential pier were slick under their feet. Billowing rolls of musty air drifted over them. Out beyond the channel, the buoys clanged rhythmically.

"Did she say cutter or sloop? What is that funny smell?"

"Smells like rotting wood."

"What is that?" Margaret stopped and pointed to the sight bursting out of the fog bank.

"No more questions. This is the slip. Come on follow me."

Before them in the fog loomed a ship creaking and thudding on the ebbing tide. She was oddly positioned at almost the bitter end of the slip. Her masts were completely enshrouded in the heavy moist yellowish cloud. It appeared as if she were sliced in half. The craft was ominously dark. Without a moment's hesitation, Edna climbed up the rope ladder that slapped out and back against her hull and crawled aboard over a misshapen gunwale. Margaret stayed down on the pier. She used her flashlight to examine the encrusted barnacles at sea level. When she looked up, she found that Edna had disappeared below decks. She pulled off a barnacle. It popped out of the side of the hull like corn off the cob. She wrapped it in a kleenex and put it into her coat pocket. She continued to examine the hull looking for identifying markings. Up under the forecastle, she thought she spotted the ship's name. It was too high up for her light to reach. She attempted to position herself at the outer side of the piling holding to the hemp line measuring a good three inches in diameter. There she almost lost her balance. She made several attempts to position herself so that she could closely examine the craft. She did this for what seemed a very long time. She had to carefully maneuver those subtle dangers - the protruding cleat, the bobbing ship, the slippery lines.

After the onset of a rustling sound, she turned to find a curious heron peering down at her from atop a piling.

"You're wintering over are you. Are you looking for your nest? You won't find it in this weather," Margaret aimed the flashlight up at the wondrous creature.

The great bird was covered with water droplets. One rolled down her beak dropping upon the dock below. The beam of light made her blink. She shook her head, then flapped her wings sending out a spray of water. With an effortless leap, she fluttered up into the mist. Margaret could hear the flap of her wings long after it disappeared.

"I think you're circling," she called out into the billowing fog bank.

Then silence drifted inland from the bay. Margaret no longer heard the clang of the channel markers. She began talking into the air.

"Why don't you come back and keep me company," she sighed. Her breath became steam.

The search began with a tinkling sound like those created by Chinese wind chimes. A strange glow appeared upon the surface of the water surrounding the ship. Margaret immediately recognized it as the red tide even though she had never seen it before. The bouncing ship slammed against the water causing the film on the tide to splash up her bow and onto her deck.

"Hello," Margaret called up to a figure she spotted on the deck. "What did you find?"

"Extinguished birthing lamps."

"What?"

"Who goes there?"

Margaret looked up and replied, "Who goes there? Me, of course. I go there. Edna stop playing games. What did you find?"

"A pretty lass if I say so myself."

Margaret aimed her flashlight toward the low pitched voice. Its luminous beam became disbursed in the particles of mist. She could barely make out the figure in the dank gloom and the relentless clouds of water vapor billowing in over the ship. It hovered over her for a long moment before moving back from the rail without sound. The red tide now splashed up over her decks and covered the railing. It rained droplets of phosphorescent beads upon the pier at Margaret's feet.

Disgusted with that trick, she turned and walked down the pier to the stern of the ship. The roundish sphere of the beam of her flashlight fell upon the pier in a steady stream as she moved. It was then she noticed the difference in the texture of the wood planks nailed into the pier and those sculpted onto the ship's hull as she swung the light up her stern. It was then she noticed the creaking and groaning of the ship as it incessantly moved up and down and then rocked side to side on the tide. It was then she noticed the ship's name painted faintly on the upper stern. Mary Dear.

"She certainly has a round bottom," Margaret muttered. "Edna. You've been on her long enough. Come on. Come on."

"Edna," she called as she climbed up the rope ladder. "You've got to get off this ship. It's the Mary Dear."

When she didn't hear anything that remotely sounded like a response, she panicked. She had absentmindedly stuffed the flash light into her sweater before grabbing onto the ladder. In those moments that followed she became as agile as a fox scampering up the ship's ropes, pulling herself over the spongy gunwale, rolling then crawling along the deck until she found the hatch to the blackened decks below. The creaking and now the grinding of the ship's frame as it listed starboard roared overhead, but during those moments she heard only a pounding in her head.

She opened the hatch with a great deal of difficulty. Despite the fact that she did not close it after her, it fell shut as soon as she reached the passageway below. The sound was dull and distant to the ear. The concave wood paneled passageway was dank. The air was almost putrid. An overhead lamp swayed back and forth with the motion of the ship. It was unlit. Light from a distant cabin reflected off its spherical glass case.

As Margaret approached, she noticed that the louvered door was shut. The light glowing from the cabin behind the door flickered even though no air was circulating. Light was coming out through the open slates in the louver.

"Edna," she called yanking at the door until it opened.

"My god woman, you look like Marley's ghost."

The outside of her raincoat was wet. Steam rolled off her slicker and her head.

"What do you mean. I've been calling and calling. Didn't you hear me? How long have you been down here?" she looked around the cabin. Stalactite like formations hung from the cracks in the cabin ceiling. The furnishings in the room were encrusted in a powdery mold. Its beams were lacy - full of worm paths and holes. The cabin was very small and had only one porthole. Margaret spotted it. She went over to it to examine the greenish brass work under the light.

"Nothing but this creaking old ship," Edna looked at her watch. "I guess I've been down here quite a while. I found an old log book," she held up a lump of ragged leather.

"Got what I want. Come on let's go," she called out into the air. She then reached up and turned the brass knob clockwise shutting off the wick.

They immediately plunged into darkness.

"What's with your flashlight."

"It was working a minute ago."

"So much for that theory."

"Batteries could be old," she hit the flashlight tube holding the batteries. They rattled inside the case. She pushed the on and off switch up and down several times. The light came back on momentarily. The dim light flickered on and off as they inched their way out into the passageway grouping along the bulkhead.

"Did you have a problem opening that door?"

"No. Why?"

"Margaret. I'll tell you later. Ha. We really don't need the flashlight. Look at the steps. Phosphorescent steps. And look at you glowing in the dark."

"Red tide has covered the marina for some reason. Unusual for this time of year. I thought it occurred only in the spring."

"A glowing microbe."

"A microbe without disease I should think. If so, we'll have serious problems with the marine life hereabouts. In fact we'll have no oyster crop this year," she called back over her shoulder. Her words were lost in the stinging wind.

Singly, they pulled themselves up onto the main deck. The sound of the great sail high up on the masts flapping above the rolling fog was almost thunderous. Margaret led the way to dockside while the percussion like sounds continued to roll in upon them incessantly in invisible sets of waves. She stopped to shine the dimming light from the flashlight up into the mainmast. Something was swinging back and forth on the rigging. From the vantage point of the deck, it looked to Margaret as if the heron had become tangled in the lines.

"So that's where you went."

She tucked the flashlight still lit and flickering into the collar of her sweater, left Edna at the railing, and climbed up the slippery rigging in an attempt to reach the bird. In a sudden calm, she was able to climb to a position where she could reach the bird. She attempted to loosen the line from around its leg and wing. She made several attempts, but the rigging was unsteady even in the temporary calm. She almost lost her balance.

While she was attempting to readjust her balance, she felt a series of yanks on the rigging. She began to descend. The wind was picking up momentum.

"Stay where you are. I'll help you free the bird."

Catching it then holding it by its legs, she managed to calm it before untangling the line to free it. With surprising ease, it managed to fly away under its own power pushing its feet against her, but without knocking her off balance. Now struggling to hold onto the frozen line, Margaret climbed back down to the deck, then down the rope ladder to the pier without further incident.

"Like those showers. Water heater was working for a change."

"That's only because I lit the pilot light."

"Anyway," Edna laughed. "Margee thank goodness you still have a key."

"And a locker," Margaret added. "Must have been six months since I last used the locker room. Doesn't look like its been used lately. I found my duck carry all. I've been looking for this for months," she held up a canvas bag.

"Aren't you going to dry your hair?"

"With what. I don't have a hair dryer," Margaret announced as they walked out onto the pier.

"Hey! My friends. What are you doing down this way?"

Edna stopped. She turned toward the figure on the pier. She pulled Margaret with her.

"We've just had a very nasty experience. This time together," she pointed to the marina community head. Her voice was muffled.

He stood on the dock leaning against a sign post. Nailed at an angle above his head barely visible in the mist swirling just above the funnel shaped light was the harbor master sign. The wood sign was hand painted. He was wearing a wool sports jacket with leather sleeves. He was smoking a pipe. The cone shaped light field that surrounded him was filled with smoke. His hair was so black that Margaret could not see the top of his head in the darkness above the rigid perimeter of the cone filled light. He wore gray wool slacks and dock siders.

CHAPTER 4

"Margaret came down to check on the house. What's your excuse Tory?" She greeted the ruggedly featured man with steel gray eyes who looked to be in his late forties with an embrace. He kissed her ear.

He did not answer her right away. He seemed to be savoring his pipe. Margaret noticed even in the dim light that his hands were meticulously manicured.

"I came down to check on the boat. We're in for some foul weather early tomorrow. Follow me. What's the latest since your last message?" he knocked his pipe against the piling.

Neither responded. Margaret was silent because she was startled to see this man and was trying to place him. Edna was silent because she was thinking how she was going to get him to investigate the recent events without paying his usual fee.

"It's an unusually warm night for this time of year wouldn't you say?" The sky overhead was beginning to clear again. The wind had died down. The fog had all but dissipated. They assumed he was making this comment based on the current and temporary weather condition. They said nothing. He waited for only a moment not really expecting a response before leading them due west down to that end of the marina.

"I got your phone message Edna. Here we are. Up this pier. I'm on the right hand side. On the bitter end."

He guided them to a French sailer with sleek lines and an unusually blunt mast. Its railings, trim and deck were teak. Once they got below deck, they found the lighted cabin warm. He was obviously planning to spend the night on the boat. Margaret took off her slicker and hung it on a hook near the galley.

"Tory, I don't think you've met my cousin Margaret." Edna spoke first. "We're on our way to dinner. Thanks," she paused and looked at Margaret. "But we'll just stay a minute."

"Yeah. We've met. A long time ago. No need for you to go out to dinner," he laughed. "I'm making spaghetti. As you can see." He turned the light on in the galley. A pot of sauce was cooking. He turned up the flame under a pot of water to bring it to a boil.

He washed his hands and dried them with a monogrammed linen towel. Then from an overhanging shelf took he took two large loaves of French bread out of their paper wrappers, sliced then buttered each piece. He put the spaghetti noodles into the boiling water.

"Eddie you'll find the silverware in the drawer."

For some reason, Edna set the captain's table without asking any questions. She methodically placed the gun handled flatware on nautical designed cotton placemats she found neatly folded in a drawer. She appeared lost in thought.

Despite her exhaustion, Margaret chatted at length about the sailing ship making a mental note that Edna knew where everything was kept. She would eventually reach a conclusion after some thought that all galleys were configured the same.

They sat down to gentle swells and to spaghetti marina with French bread and a spinach and egg salad. He waited until the last minute to pour on the raspberry vinegar dressing. It changed the color of the thinly sliced egg whites. For a time, they ate in silence. This silence remained only until the ship's clock rang four bells. This sound acted as a reminder for them to begin the very first phase of the investigation process.

"We'll fill you in on what we've learned today," Edna began.

"Who is this Max character," he interrupted at one point.

"Maxim Barrier. He's a partner or was in the antique shop in South Beach."

"He still is a partner," Edna corrected. "That's the current problem."

"You're right. He's an interesting guy. His father used to work in the old flour mill down at the foot of M Street. You know the area where the railroad tracks end at the river under the viaduct. I think the old mill functioned as a mill until it was gutted and refurbished just a couple of years ago. It's now a condo."

"Next to the tannery. Remember the sign? It was painted on the side of the tannery. It was something like - the odors you smell are not coming from this building. Ha. Ha. If they weren't coming from the tannery, they must have been coming from the old mill."

"Maxim. Yes. He had a pretty successful career. He wound up as attorney general in American Canal Zone or some such exotic place. He came back from that tour to find that his wife had left him. I think he was surprised. I think he was surprised because she was with him on that tour and had gone home to get the house in order or some such thing. All of that was in his previous life before he retired and bought the antique shop."

"Which one?"

"Which one what?"

"Which antique shop. Never mind. For now it's not important. I've heard the name before. In fact, I know I've run into that guy somewhere," he got up and went to his desk at the port side of the galley. It consisted of a part of the galley counter, a set of pull down cabinets that hung over it and canvas captain's chair.

"I met him only once. That happened a long time ago. Heard a lot about him over the years though. Where did I meet him."

"Margaret even if the swinging corpse was Max. You may be able to recognize him."

"First thing we've got to do is to get a picture of this joker," he said through his teeth.

"Why?"

"So that Margaret can get a look at his puss," he had a habit of spitting out his words. He was impatient.

"Why else?" Edna shrugged.

"The corpse I saw hanging this morning had a bloated misshapen face."

"Ugh," Edna continued with her monologue for some minutes. Margaret made no further attempt to add or change any information.

"Now wait a minute. Wait a minute. You going to tell me with a straight face that you boarded a sloop parked here in this marina," he interrupted after some minutes into Edna's monologue pointing to the deck with the thrust of his forefinger.

"I didn't say anything about a sailing ship. Did I," Edna mused.

"I did, but that was twenty minutes ago," remarked Margaret. She was twirling the spaghetti on her fork using her plate to balance her fork, not the conventional spoon. She took off her glasses then picked up the bottle of salad dressing and turned it to read the triangular label on the back of the bottle.

"Like this walnut and raspberry vinegar. Edna leapt over the side of that ship like a gazelle. I really don't think I've ever seen anything quite like it. What did you think of her?"

"What? Edna leaping like a gazelle?" he was sprinkling parmesan cheese on Edna's spaghetti sauce.

"The Island packet, my friend."

"Island packet you say. I've yet to see a packet hereabouts." he passed around the roll basket filled with sliced garlic bread.

"Come on. You saw it."

"Ok then. I did not see a packet. OK. We'll go out after dinner to take a look."

"Yeah. When you walk us to the car."

Margaret did not pick up on this signal. She was concentrating on identifying the packet.

"The green bomber."

"Don't laugh. Margaret is down here with Chester's playpen -- the truck. Ha. Ha. OK Margaret. We need to go over in great detail just exactly what you found this morning."

"I was out jogging with Chester. It was about sunrise. Very late this time of year."

"Chester is the dog. What time would you say?" Edna winked at Tory.

"Sevenish. The sun was over the horizon. Wind was up. We were jogging by the marina."

"This one?"

"Yes. I decided not to go down to that little cafe in South Beach that opens early , because they don't get doughnuts in until around nine. But the deli across the road here has a regular kitchen so I was going to jog to the deli, eat some breakfast and job off the breakfast."

"It's closed in the winter."

"Yes it is closed, but just until noon. How disappointing. Anyway, as we jogged past the marina something happened. I suspect something happened anyway. Chester, in the meantime, began acting very peculiarly. He ran into the marina and down onto the pier. I followed naturally. You know I'm very near sighted. I was practically upon the Saber before I saw this sack of something hanging from the mast. "

"Are you sure it wasn't actually a sack of something or maybe a torn sail?"

"I'm sure. For one thing it had a green face and a purple tongue. It was like a stuffed scarecrow," she shuddered.

Tory spontaneously got up, went to Margaret, and put his arm around her shoulder. She sighed.

"What does that tell you?" Edna asked with a mouth full of spaghetti.

"Well for one thing, the corpse may have been hanging there a while."

"Ugly. Ugly."

"And for another?"

"At this juncture, I can only guess. A couple of scenarios come to mind. It could have been an accident. We had a severe storm the other night. Someone could have come down to the marina, planning to spend the night on the boat. Found the sails had gotten loose and somehow simply got tangled up in a billowing sail. Maybe he tripped over a line."

"Unlikely, since the boat was moved," Edna proposed.

"It is likely only if the corpse was not a corpse, but say the sails got caught up in the rigging in such that the bundle looked like man. Boats move in and out of this marina frequently. Less frequently in winter. You have no other witnesses."

"Chester."

"He may prove to be a good witness. However, he may not. Let's look at the original scenario. Suppose it was a corpse you saw. Why was it in such an advanced state?"

"I don't know.."

"Or Blackbeard's head."

"What?" asked Margaret while buttering a slice of French bread.

"In a well worn out phase, a warning to all that this fate will be yours if you are the enemy."

"Let's suppose that someone was actually murdered. Why would the murder victim be hung out on mast instead of being stuffed in the ship's hole? It most likely for a purpose. An insidious one. If we are dealing with some sort of cartel, we're going to need to do a couple of things. First track any like kind activity, do some analysis and then identify just what we're dealing with."

"What is a cartel?"

"Like I just said a warning to one and all not to do whatever the victim did to infuriate those running the cartel. Margaret a cartel is like a business conglomerate. Only made up of a group of them. It has the personality of a monopoly," Edna was becoming impatient.

"Isn't this whole thing at the very least medieval?

"Margaret, I think the word is Byzantine. Why do you think we're dealing with a cartel Tory?"

"From just what you've said."

"You mean Margaret's friend Max?"

"That certainly is a familiar name. Wait a minute. I think it's coming to me. Wasn't he married to Eustacia," Margaret got up and snapped her fingers.

"Eustacia the first wife of a string of wives," Edna conjectured.

"That's right. He was in law school or was he clerking in a law firm when they married. The wedding of the century. If I remember correctly, she was six or seven years older than he. Wasn't her father the real estate magnate who made his fortune during the fifties only to lose it when she was a teenager. She was raised in one of those old stone mansions that straddles the park."

"Wasn't there a scandal?"

"What?" Tory took out a small notebook and made some notes.

"Tory you weren't around town at the time."

"The scandal was about her family. The old aunt. She was put into St. E's. That part of the puzzle was more in the line of a skeleton in the closet than a scandal."

"Margaret I never knew about that."

"Of course. How could you? I only knew because of Peaches. Eustacia's worst enemy in high school. She was old money; Peaches was a social climber. Peaches' mother looked like a truck driver and worked."

"What does that have to do with anything."

"It was the old aunt who owned the house. Eustacia's aunt. Somehow by hook or by crook - her father mortgaged that place to the hilt. I think is was to finance a series of real estate ventures. Then he went bust. He was a friend of one of the restaurateurs uptown. He was killed crossing the avenue in front of the restaurant. A hit and run."

"Who was killed?"

"Eustacia's father. Someone with diplomatic tags. I don't think Max really wasn't affected by any of that. Maybe some old debts."

"Maybe he set up the whole scheme."

"But Tory when they divorced, Eustacia's financial interests had long since dissipated. He gave her a small settlement and went off to marry his secretary."

"He and Eustacia had six kids. He put them all in private schools. I don't think the settlement was small. And no. It wasn't his secretary. It was some one else's wife," Edna was adamant.

"I'm not sure what she was or who she was. Anyway, she - wife number 2 - was at least twenty years younger. She never really recovered. I think she went into a decline."

"Not changing the subject radically, but what about the senator?" Edna asked.

"Oh yes. You're quite right. That is another story," Margaret sighed.

"What about the senator?" echoed Tory.

"I think that's part of another scandal. He used to pal around with Eustacia's father. He had a sister who was a society columnist. Anyway they all used to meet at Valduce's...."

"Where is Valduce's?" Tory asked.

"The one uptown on the avenue."

"The owner of Valduce's being the old man's friend."

"Did they have a dining room in the back garden?" laughed Edna.

"I don't know Edna. You mean the little garden lined with the white rose covered trellis. Probably did when the weather was not too cold or too hot."

"And the senator?" Tory was persistent in his questions.

"This is where the scandal comes in. I think it all began when the Senator lost money in one of old man McSwiny's real estate ventures. At least his troubles surfaced some time afterwards. I can't be absolutely certain that is how or where his money troubles got started. And those problems could have always been there or maybe as he aged his business acumen diminished."

"Anyway, he made some bad business decisions which led to what exactly."

"A desire to recoup from his financial losses," speculated Edna. She turned and grinned at Tory.

"More than likely. Someone on the state elections board filed a complaint."

"An irregularity was spotted."

"That's putting it mildly Tory. Justice sent out a task force to gather documentation of all sorts. I think it included collecting affidavits too. The story goes that all of the documentation collected was put into the local court house. Very shortly thereafter the court house burnt to the ground. The task force was called back to Washington. End of probe," Margaret shrugged.

"What makes your story interesting is what you've left out," Tory began. "Let's take a look at this scenario for just a minute," he looked at Edna who was about to speak.

"Correct me if I'm wrong. What we have here is a very senior senator. A man who has made his career in politics. He most likely was ready to retire when he discovers that his investments have turned sour or maybe worse. He has made enemies over the years back home. A challenger is perched ready to run against him and has enough ammunition to discredit the senator. The challenger gets someone of like kind on the elections board to report the irregularity to Justice. This brings forth the investigation. The senator, however, is not without friends and supporters, who do some pretty wild stuff."

"Like what?"

"Like locally. Someone burned down the court house. I'm sure it was not an accident. And, it sounds like Justice called off the investigation either because the documentation was critical to the case or if the witnesses were critical - they disappeared or recanted their statements. Either way the investigation was too expensive to continue."

"Perhaps someone on the hill pulled out the task force."

"If you mean for political reasons - very unlikely. Even though the good old boy network plays a major role in all of this. He might have had some favors due...."

"Now look. Only two reasons that I can think of would have impacted on deeojays decision - the hill or cost," Edna pursued. "I just want to pull in Max for a minute. He probably went before the ethics committee with the argument that the senator was innocent of all charges preferred by the election board and would not seek reelection."

"Which is French for the task force really didn't uncover all that much or the senator is not going to run again so why go to the expense of continuing this investigation," Edna interrupted.

"Except that the evidence was destroyed. I think that the reason the story even surfaced, because it was not carried here in the press except for maybe a three paragraph notice...."

"You think they did uncover something."

"Thanks for thinking for me. Yes, I do. And even though the hit-and-run happened, he was making preparations to run again."

"Margaret how do you know that."

"Eustacia."

"Where was Max."

"He was around. Eustacia just had her sixth child. He was killed just before the christening. The senator and her father, too I guess, not Max."

"Why would you remember that?" Edna was finishing off the loaf of bread.

"I don't know why. It happened so long ago," Margaret bit her lip.

"This Max character carries a lot of baggage."

"Carried," mused Edna.

"So you think it was Max hanging from the yardarm."

"He's definitely missing."

"Yes," Margaret agreed. "But I think that it has been a while. Didn't Don say something to that effect?"

"Did he? No. I don't think he did."

"Who?"

"Dan MacIntosh. He is Max's partner in the antique shop venture. Dan is the one who told us about Max dropping off the face of the earth."

"Just this afternoon," Tory reiterated.

"But he didn't say when," Margaret was insistent.

"Correct me Eddie if I'm wrong. You're making a major assumption. That assumption is that you believe it - the corpse - is Max. You believe it is Max, because Max's partner Don stated to you this afternoon that Max has disappeared."

"Max definitely disappeared from Dan's life," Margaret added. "What I saw hanging from the yardarm could have been someone else."

"Could have been. But he was hanging from a boat that matches the description of Max's boat docked in Max's very own slip."

"So he owned a Saber. That's what you spotted in the harbor master's office."

"Yep. The old ship's chart. We are dealing in a shadowy world," Edna added.

"With shadowy figures. Max's profile is an interesting one. You don't happen to remember which law firm he was with...."

"Segurar and Camara. Why?"

"How did you know that Eddie?

"I don't know. It was just something everyone knew. I think it's the only law firm on Porter Street," Edna got up stretched and yawned.

"You two are what is known - in some circles," he lowered his voice, "as power watchers."

"Oh yeah. You can't but help it in this town. Everyone has a skeleton or two in the closet. The people in this town, however, are high profile. So when something happens, it is usually picked up by the press...."

"In a casual sort of way," Margaret added.

"Tell me about the law firm."

"Tory. I don't know too much about S and C except that locally - the Washington office was founded during FDR's administration as a specialty office. That is to say, it specialized in inter and intra state commerce litigation."

"It most likely dealt with one of the old sunset commissions."

"S and C did and still does. On that particular sunset commission; however, the sun never set. At times it - the commission - was supposed to disappear. But it simply never did. In fact one of the last administration's major scandals surfaced in order to put the administration's order to begin its shutdown on hold. And on top of that, I think Max was in the Congressional liaison division."

It was obvious Edna's information on the topic was encyclopedic.

"Where else would he have been? Where else? He must have had incredible political pull," Tory was pacing back and forth.

"We don't have to waste time on that issue. He was most likely the mastermind behind ferreting out that particular administration's scandal. The name of the game is -- if you uncover a scandal, you get the winnings. That is to say, you get to name the size and kind of winnings."

"Yes, precisely. But what is the pattern we are unfolding here and there...."

"But before we get into that," Margaret interrupted. "What was the administration scandal that was so devastating that it crippled the administration's efforts to shut down the old commercial commission?"

"Correction Margaret. It was only a stalling tactic until the next presidential election. By the time the election came and went, the impetus to shut down the commission had either been put on a back burner or neglected until it was forgotten or died. It certainly was never played up in the press. And on top of that, the newly elected president was of the same party. He or at least his advisors had no interest in revisiting either the scandal or the problems that surfaced during the investigation and conveniently forgot about the shutdown of the commission."

"Yes," Tory was becoming impatient.

"I can't remember off the top of my head."

"It might be the key to the whole thing."

"Yes. It might. It will come to me eventually."

"Tory you were saying there appears to be a pattern of some sort."

"Yes. Don't you see it? Your friend Max. Let's look at this character for a minute."

"We all know he came from an obscure working class background. He married her for her money. Only she was all out," Margaret was indignant.

"Not so. She might have been all out when he finished with her, but she was not when they married," Edna reminded Margaret. "Anyway a large part of her wealth was the incredible number of contacts her father had. And on top of that Eustacia was not nouveau riche."

"What? What I need is a drink." Margaret was about to pour a little wine into her water glass when Tory handed her a wine glass.

"Of course. Of course I knew that. He was from West Virginia. A small town boy. A wheeler dealer who made it big. I'm tired. It's been a long day. Let's get back. Chester has to be let out."

CHAPTER 5

Margaret got up, made her bed, a daily ritual consisting of simply pulling up the comforter puffed in a baffle karostep stitch over flannel sheets, and dressed by the converted ship's lamp in the pre dawn darkness. This morning she decided to change the musty sheets. She put them in a wicker basket and placed them at the top of the stairs. She descended intending to brew a pot of coffee while she showered. Instead of showering; however, she pulled on her dark gray jogging suit and black knit cap and took Chester out for a run. At first, he was unwilling to go outside. He reluctantly climbed out of his basket, warmed by the kitchen furnace, to first stretch, yawn, shake his head, drink rusty water, and sniff Margaret's leg.

The night sky overhead had remained cloudless during that short duration between dinner hours and the coming of dawn. Fringes of the milky way still burst through that dark edge of the atmosphere out toward the eastern shoreline.

She jogged on the roadside carefully balancing her steps along the lowest edge of the bowed road pavement and the ditches that straddled it. They again entered the marina. This morning they entered through the back entrance - the entrance nearest the roadside. Margaret decided to jog along the edge of the pier only after Chester picked up his ears, growled, and trotted off onto the gravel entrance road. Margaret quieted him with a series of verbal commands. She followed Chester at some distance. He decidedly picked up his pace and then ran to a cluster of wooden plank buildings not far from the harbor master complex. He stood whining and growling as she approached. The moon still cast a shadow.

"Eddie."

"What?"

She was pulled into the shadows of the out buildings behind the dumpster. Chester sat growling.

"Eddie. Keep that dog quiet."

"Come here Chester. Here boy." He trotted into the deep shadows panting loudly.

"Look due east. At the end of the pier. It just pulled out of the slip where you found the Saber," he whispered into her ear.

"How can I look when you're nuzzling the back of my neck."

He did not answer. She could tell he was not listening to what she had to say.

The Saber had on only its running lights. Several figures were seen walking about on its aft deck. Margaret concentrated on trying to identify their faces. The ship was too far away.

"Something is coming in and out all right," he was whispering into her ear. He pulled her up against him. Chester was whining at her feet.

"Oh my. Who are they?"

"Could be members of the yacht club, but maybe not. Whoever they are they're delivering stuff off that Saber. Did a truck pass you on the roadside?" she could only see the misty breath.

"Not down my way. What kind of a truck."

"A small one."

"I'll keep an eye out," Margaret thought this response to her question was incredibly stupid. She decided to give him a equally stupid response. However, she became frightened at the sight of the ape like men aboard the Sprint.

He kissed her ear. "Go ahead and continue jogging. I think you were spotted."

"Now look Tory I'm not...."

"Go on. Vite. Vite," he released her head with his hands. "I might be in danger. I've seen too much."

"What about me?" she adjusted her cap.

"What? Oh hell. I'm going to follow her as soon as she clears the marina."

They jogged back down the gravel drive to the roadside. Chester was sulking. He bounced along with his tail between his hind legs. Margaret stopped at the fence line and turned to watch the yacht. Out beyond them in the channel the Saber Sprint with the running lights now turned low, not quite visible from the shore moved out with the morning tide like a ghost ship. Her little outboard engine barely made a sound.

The shower water was tepid and hard. It left brown stains on the shower stall that never came out. The soap bar never quite lathered and the soap foam she did manage to lather on her skin was difficult to wash off. Because the water situation was so grim, Margaret always brought her own water to drink. She stored it on old plastic milk bottles in gallon and half gallon sizes.

"Tell me just how did you meet this guy?"

Margaret was standing on the enclosed glass porch. She had just put down her cup of coffee and was peering nervously out onto the Bay with her binoculars. The sky was filled with upside down ruffled clouds that were shaped in rows of red mountain peaks defined by black valleys.

"At a tea fight?"

"A what?"

"A Saturday afternoon tea fight."

"You mean the Sunday afternoon tea fights. You're kidding."

"No I'm not. He was part of the old upward bound program. So he was older than the other middies."

"Upward from what?"

"Grass roots. He's a grass roots kind of guy."

"In a common sort of way."

"What did you say Margaret."

"I said you can certainly say that again."

"Don't knock him. He retired as a commander."

"Commander. What was his specialty?"

"NIS."

"The old NIS."

"An echo? Yes. West Coast."

"I guess he's seen some pretty grizzly stuff in his time. That's probably why he makes such a good PI," Margaret took a long, thoughtful sip of coffee from her English tea cup. She was trying to measure Edna's reactions to her probe.

"We've given him a lot of business over the past couple of years. He always delivers. He sure can come up with a profile."

"What does he investigate exactly."

"Mostly industrial espionage. That's his particular specialty. You know his last tour out was in San Pedro. Apparently a lot of stuff went on down at 32nd Street."

"That place is strictly for refitting."

"Refitting. Oh yeah. The pier down on thirty-second street. As the fleet comes in and goes out. They've got to refit. But that's not all they do."

"So you called him in."

"Yes I did Margaret. And he said as much last night. I don't want to sound defensive. However," she began -- her voice trailed off. "I wasn't expecting him to surface so soon. I think that was accidental. He probably did just come down to check the boat. He could be between jobs. And he thinks that you've stumbled onto something pretty big."

"Can you give me a profile?"

"On Tory?"

Margaret said nothing. The sky was changing color from hazy cobalt to deep red to pale blue.

"Seems to me I've heard a story or two about him along time ago. During the war before his NIS days, he was a seal. What was it now. Let me think," she left the porch abruptly.

"I think he was part of the team that mined Haiphong harbor. Very dangerous work. Most of that team did not come back," she walked back onto the porch and without skipping a beat she continued.

"You're right about checking on the boat," Margaret interrupted. "He must come down at least once a month during the winter. And by the looks as to how its outfitted, maybe more often. But our problem is still speculation at this point. I think it's too early to tell...."

"I don't think we should take any chances. Now look I've got to get back to the office. How long are you going to be down here?"

"Just through the weekend I think. Why?"

"Tory can keep an eye on this place for you."

Margaret frowned.

"Even when you're not here. Only until this current problem blows over. Believe me this guy is harmless."

"I got news for you Edna," Margaret then changed her mind. "This problem may be long term. There may be smugglers about."

"That's a different problem. Let's focus on the murder. It might very well be the key."

"But the key to what? Do we really want to find out what is going on," Margaret sighed.

"I'm afraid when a murder is involved, we must do what we must do."

"But I've done my duty I've informed the police. Besides I'm getting hives."

"Shall we get into a philosophical discuss about the rights and responsibilities of citizens?"

"Please no more half words. I'm getting a headache and indigestion on top of the hives. I'm not sure I want to be a part of this whole thing any longer."

"Who is that hunk walking around the side of the house?"

He sauntered across the community owned road, now filled with a huge ancient oak and a set of its offspring, looking out across toward the Tillman Islands group. The frost covered ground crunched under his shoes.

"I think it's the young police officer I saw yesterday. Doesn't he take your breath away."

"Good morning. Won't you come in?" Margaret called as she opened the glass pained door.

"Good morning."

"Officer. This is my sister Edna."

"Hello. I'm Jim McNearny." He turned to Margaret, "We've got a few more questions for you."

"Of course. Be happy to answer any questions you've got."

Those questions were the same ones he asked the morning before. Margaret made sure she rephrased every piece of information she spoke, because in substance she could provide no further information and felt it critical that her observations appeared credible. He was about to sit on one of a pair of matching wicker chairs.

"Don't sit there. The leg is broken," Edna directed him to the couch facing the bay. She sat in the fauteuil. Then she sat on the porch bench.

He seated himself on the yellow wicker couch, sinking into overstuffed chintz cushions, and immediately began taking notes interrupted only by Edna first bringing him coffee then a refill. She leaned over to turn on the marble lamp and to get a closer look at his list of questions.

At one point during one of the interruptions, Margaret got up from the Victorian garden bench with its rounded arms and bowed legs that she painted celery in a fit of pique to pick up the binoculars. Without speaking she began searching the bay scape for the two sail boats. She had almost forgotten. She spotted first Tory's boat then she found the Saber below it on the bay at the far southern end of her line of sight. They were almost out of view despite the fact the bay was windless on this bitter cold morning. Everything appeared calm. Relieved, she put down the binoculars.

"What's out there Margaret?"

"I'm sorry. What did you say?" she turned and glared at Edna, who was arranging the teapot and creamer on the tray.

"Would you like some more coffee."

"Why. Yes."

"Here is your big English tea cup. What's out there that's got your interest up?"

Margaret absentmindedly took the cup leaving the saucer, drank some of the coffee, put the cup directly on the toll painted tray that she used as an end table and sat unceremoniously into the chintz cushion next to the young man. She would occasionally lean over to the end table to pick up the cup, drink from it and the put it back while answering the repetitive questions. At a critical point in the conversation, she put on her glasses to read the notes he was preparing. She was so intent on reading the notes that she leaned across his arm in order to add or delete words or phrases to his notes with his pen that it was a full twenty minutes before he said anything.

'Ma'am. I don't think you're supposed to change...."

"I'm not changing anything, but adding points for emphasis."

"Yes. But...."

"I've clearly marked it in pen. See. When you type it up, you can certainly change it back or just do whatever you want. But I feel that accuracy in reporting is essential to good reporting. Or perhaps even the most critical element during the investigative process. Don't you agree? Here comes more coffee."

Margaret paused at this strategic point. She was afraid she was overstepping some imaginary boundary line. She made her foray waiting to hear a strong protest. Thus far, no strong protest surfaced. He seemed content to simply ask and the re ask the same set of questions.

About an hour later, Edna again entered the porch. This time in the blazing sunlight, she carried a silver tray filled with a china pot of coffee and creamer of lime green and a white china basket of blueberry muffins wrapped in an old starched linen napkin edged in Battenberg lace. She placed the tray on the tea cart with a flourish. She moved about fussing over setting the china on the tea cart with the demeanor of a mid Victorian matriarch. She then carefully moved the tray to center it upon the wicker tea cart. The silver reflected the sunlight flashing light up under her chin and on her neck. Then she moved the ancient tea cart strategically across the painted wood floor crossing the wide border of hand painted flowers and its background of green leaves only once so as not the mark the decorative border. She moved it from the swing side of the porch to the cluster of wicker furniture stuffed with over sized puffed cushions in plaid and flower prints. She had an eye for arranging furniture. She decided to give this setting what she considered a complete definition by adding to the antique rug underfoot, the neglected potted fern and the nondescript painted coffee table.

She reached up to turn on the fan to rotate it in a backward motion. She filled her cup with coffee and two percent milk and put one of the sliced muffin halves on the side of gold rimmed Havilland saucer. After this flurry of activity, which went unnoticed, she sat in the plaid cushion tied with grosgrain ribbon to the back rung of the rocker. She pulled up her calf length kaki skirt, placing her booted feet upon the crocheted foot stool. It was covered with a black tapestry and filled with Victorian flowers. She carefully placed her lace napkin on her lap. She appeared almost majestic. Meticulously, she dabbed the corners of her mouth with her napkin after nibbling and before talking. She began as soon as she noticed that the interview was almost finished.

Chester came out to the porch to sit in the corner by the space heater. He was chewing on an old shoe.

From that point on during their discourse the intricate path of the interview characterized by its all but undetected ebb and flow, Edna became more intrusive. Her hovering took hold and intensified. It was as though, she was going through a process variable consisting of taking the information and processing it simultaneously with those unlike or even like kind bits and pieces that happened to surface during the course of the conversation. At various points, she would verbally make an observation. She did this using both Margaret's and the young officer's words as points of reference. If they agreed with or made no comment concerning her remarks, she went on with this indefinite process of moving to the next step. If they did not agree, however, she would stall the process until she was able to formulate a conclusion. The bulk of this maneuvering effort she was able to accomplish quickly and effortlessly for several reasons. She had no preset boundaries within which to encase her set of observations. And at this early stage she knew that the incident as reported was still not verifiable so she gave herself some latitude in forming her questions.

With that in mind, she decided to phrase a single set of her questions in a series of hypotheticals. She soon gave up however. The young officer could make no germane response. It appeared the investigative team assigned to this case knew little or nothing beyond Margaret's unverifiable report, but she was not sure at this juncture.

As for Margaret, she continued not only to respond in a vague manner, but to glare openly at Edna. At times they would talk in low tones ignoring Edna as much as possible. Margaret would softly repeat a phrase after moving close to his left ear. He would look up occasionally from his writing task to search her face. They would discuss a phrase or a term at some length before deciding how to place that information into the body of the report.

"Now wait...," she would say. "I'm not sure...."

Edna suddenly became bored with her idea, looked at her watch, picked up the tray and left the porch. On her way to the kitchen, she let Chester out to wander up and down bay front.

Exuberant at nothing in particular, he decided to chase a pair of mallards, who themselves had decided to winter over this particular season. He gingerly ran out onto the rocks under the pier and, in general, made a nuisance of himself. After a few hops and jumps, they took flight to roost until noon time up on the pilings jutting out from the point.

He came back into the house as the police officer left through the porch door. He crossed between them through the doorway scampering across the porch to pick up the shoe. He came back to Margaret dropping it at her feet where he sat thumping his wet tail on the floor where he marked the flower imprinted border with sand.

"Please call me if you find out anything new," he said as he came close to her and spoke into her ear.

Margaret was about to answer when she became distracted by Chester thumping his tail on her leg, picking up the shoe, and then dropping it on her foot. She looked down then up into his face. He put his pen in his shirt pocket and said.

"If anything comes up, please call me."

"Margaret."

"Let me have your card. I'll call you. Yes Edna," she turned to answer.

"I put one on the table. I don't want to alarm you, but...."

"OK. OK."

She closed the glass door and, after a long minute, took the shoe from Chester.

"What do you have in your hand?" Edna came out onto the porch. She went to the windows facing north to watch the officer get into a county car and back it down to the gravel access road.

"Edna. This is the shoe Chester brought back with him yesterday morning."

"From where?"

"From the marina, " she put her glasses on. "Look it's man's dock sider size ten and a half. It's new. I think he got it from the deck of the Saber."

"We now know two things for certain. A Saber exists. Tory can ID her. Once we do that we can find registered ownership."

"That's what I've been following all morning," Edna continued. "However, if the yacht we spotted in slip seventeen is indeed the Saber or whatever model you saw yesterday then why was it brought back? Where is the corpse? And now this shoe."

"Yes the shoe."

"Well what about the shoe?"

"From the corpse. It must have fallen off the corpse."

CHAPTER 6

"I can't think of what it is."

"What?"

"There is something else. I'll remember it. But first I'm going to Hank's."

"Hank's."

"The new laundromat. I get a sense of self worth sorting through laundry. And while I'm doing the laundry, I'm going to ask around the neighborhood." Margaret was standing by the fireplace counting the quarters in her change purse. She took it out of her maroon Avionne purse and put the quarters, one by one, on the white colonial mantel under the brass game cock. Sunlight strewn in through the open slats of the Venetian blinds running vertically across the windows at the back of the living room. Streams of light shown across the Williamsburg green wall behind the fireplace at an angle.

"Be sure to phrase your questions carefully. Maybe somebody remembers seeing the guy when he was alive." Edna was putting together the canister vacuum cleaner. She had on a gingham apron.

"Or maybe someone will tell me something that I don't already know," Margaret went to the closet in the second bedroom off the living room and pulled out a dust mop. She had the habit of mopping first and then vacuuming. Edna did not seem to notice the flurry of activity Margaret had undertaken to quickly mop under the bed then in the dining room, then in the living room along the walls and under the tables and bookcases.

"Let's review a set of questions. But first we must have a goal in mind."

"The goal is to be unobtrusive."

"If we can get some answers to questions that appear to be benign then we've really gotten somewhere. That's what I'll do. I'll create a set of benign questions, not for a better word penetrating, not obnoxious, but earnestly benign."

"How can you say that? Every question is obnoxious."

"Not if it is done tastefully."

"Horse hockey. Not if what is done tastefully. Interrogation? An interrogation tastefully done. That's rich."

"OK. OK. However, I wouldn't use such a strong word for the gentle probing that you are about to undertake."

"Edna. I will probe, but I get to pick time and place and how to do it."

"One of the major points I want to make to is for you to seriously consider taking in more information than you give out."

"That's a pretty tough rule. Especially for someone like myself. I have no clout ," Margaret complained. "I always have to compromise."

"I probably won't be here when you get back," Edna sounded disjointed. "If I get a chance, I'll come down in a couple of days. I don't think Hank's is the new laundromat. It's the old one. The new laundromat is down across from Ernie's on the channel."

"That's right, however, I want to go to Hank's. It's across the street from the antique shop. I will call you tonight. You can give me your set of logically thought out questions over the phone. Come on Chester," she called over the sound of the vacuum cleaner. She took the mop outside and shook it behind the garage and leaned it upside down against the inside of the fence.

After stopping at the corner cafe to pick up bottle of lime flavored water and a chicken salad sandwich, Margaret decided to be as discrete as possible. She drove down the back street and parked behind the laundromat instead of driving down the main road and parking in front. Hank's was housed in one of a cluster of single story buildings lining the main street. Set along the street front in a helter skelter fashion, these facades faced due east. Any view of the bay was blocked by the antique shop building directly cars the street and the row of cottages squeezed into half lots just beyond a cluttered alley.

She went in through the screen door, torn open at the lower left hanging at an angle, past the newly repaired hot water heater to find the dollar changer.

"Chester go take a water break."

He returned to bang on the back door. Margaret went back to open it after hastily putting down the double stacked baskets on the heavily scuffed linoleum floor. Chester trotted into the laundromat brushing past her legs to the front window to sit watching for seagulls or a stray cat.

"Hi." a young woman appeared from behind a row of dryers. She was wearing a white sweat shirt over gravel washed kakis and white jogging shoes. Her hair was wound around large plastic curlers.

"Hi. There," Margaret called lifting the baskets from the floor and putting them on top of one of the a stainless steel washers. "Where's Bernice?"

"Everybody's askin' for Bernice. She's down to her mother's for a while."

"When will she be back?" Margaret walked to the back of the laundromat to the Formica counter. She put a five dollar bill on the counter. And while patiently waiting for change, she decided to leaf through a pile of posted notices layered one on top of the other. She read each one quickly and stopped only when she spotted a notice dated the previous summer.

"I guess after she gets better," the young woman opened an army green fishing tackle box and brought out a roll of five dollars worth of quarters. "Be sure and count those quarters."

"Say tell me what you know about this notice. It's real old," she pulled it out from near the bottom of the pile of papers laying on top of the cracked end of the Formica counter.

"Bernice likes to save those. I guess she won't care that you're messin' up her stuff. What is it for?"

"Well let's see. It's some kind of a notice or advertisement for a party. It reads 'BYOB Saturday, July 10. 302 South Eads.' Why does that address ring a bell?" she lied.

"Let me see that.," the young blond woman picked up the notice. "I think that's the sheriff's address. Ones't a year he gives a BYOB party. It usually lasts two days. He lives in Tankersly's old house straight at the top of the hill from here. It was really run down if you know what I mean. Living room ceiling had fallen in. He fixed it up mostly on the outside though. My mother lives just across the street. She goes over there to pick peaches in August and apples in September. She cans a lot. He just put in running water and an oil furnace. He don't have no wife."

"Never did?"

"Did once. I think."

"Had running water just once?" Margaret wanted to avoid any appearance that she was asking questions about the sheriff. However, she knew it was useless to expect that the young woman did not notice what she was interested in or who was the center of her questions.

"Oh that. He has a well. He capped it though."

"Everyone down here in town has city water don't they?"

"Yeah. We had city water put in five years ago."

"We're fighting for it up our way."

"Where are you?"

"Up in the park."

"Everybody up your way on well and septic?"

"Everyone. Even those people on the wetlands side of the road. Now tell me about Bernice. For one thing she and her mother don't get along and another her mother lives down past Pax river. Why would she go all the way down there."

"Bernice is not doing so good. She got a gunshot to the chest."

"What?"

"Yeah. Her old man walked in the other night and gave her one hell of a blast."

"Why would he do that? I just saw her yesterday. She was here."

"Well. I had to go to town with the kids," she sounded defensive. "She ought'nave come in. Anyway she ain't gonna be comin' around here for a while."

"I think she really needs this job. Let me have her mother's phone number would you."

"Don't think I got it."

"Oh good hell," Margaret went back to begin sorting and loading clothes into the washing machines. She did not speak again until each bundle was placed in a separate machine and the soap dispensed. She shut the top lids or the side cylindrical doors inserting quarters into the slots in succession. She sat down to leaf through the north county paper and to watch the street traffic. It happened during the rinse cycle. She noticed the young woman was standing in the front window. She was watching two men crossing the street on the diagonal. They walked down the sidewalk on the far side.

Margaret decided to put on her horned rimmed glasses and move closer to the front window. She started when she recognized them as the two men she sat behind in the restaurant. They stood on the sidewalk and talked and then went into the antique shop through its entrance directly across the street. Before entering the building, they looked up and down the street. She did not recognize them initially because she had only gotten a glimpse of them in the restaurant. Today they had on hunting gear. These outfits greatly altered their appearance.

"Bernice. Is it duck hunting season?"

"I'm not Bernice. I'm Alicia."

"Sorry. Alicia. When does it start?"

"Like every year. Started last Friday. Say you know... one of them guys was after Bernice." Alicia came to the front of the laundromat from the furnace room. Margaret pulled up her white wool socks under her sweat pants.

"Was he the one pestering her last summer?"

"Don't know. Maybe. He don't come around very often."

"I'll be back in a minute. I hope you've got hot water this year. Would you put my stuff in the dryer? I left some quarters on the counter. Chester stay. Don't mind Chester. He'll protect you while I'm gone. Just let him out when he needs a water break."

Chester sat at the sunny window thumping his tail on the cement floor. He turned to whimper, but turned again to look through the dusted rain streaks. He caught sight of the men leaving the shop and heading toward the post office. He growled.

* * *

The house was intriguing despite the fact it was rectangular in shape, the shape of a soda cracker box, and nondescript in style and color. She spent a good part of an hour walking the perimeter and over the gravel paths through the dormant gardens. Despite the fact that everything inhabiting that landscape was now starkly skeletal except for a few evergreens, she found the gardens still as vibrant as in summer. She examined the dwarf fruit trees on a lower terrace and its boundary rock garden. It appeared to host a floating garden. The horizontal crevices streaking its rock face were filled with mosses and wormwort and Serbian bellflower.

She sat for a while on a stone mushroom she found planted upon a neatly formed gravel base consisting of good size chunks of stone. She found herself walking through the remnants of the back garden, twisted and dried out raspberry vines, yellow corn stalks, dug up rows now covered with straw. This path lead her to the open gazebo. She inspected its construction of intricately turned posts and hand hewn cross beams. Clay pots placed upside down were neatly stacked here and there. One side of it was used as a grape arbor. She ran her fingers along the grape vines now without fruit, leafless and gray. Its twisted vines were exposed.

She walked along the brick path deep in thought carrying the remains of a stalk of purple honeybells she found under a dormant hosta. Its wilted leaves surrounded clumps of white coneflowers and northern purple gayfeather. It led her to the foot of the back stairs. Primitively made, the staircase consisted of a set of five steps. Each step was formed by nailing together two planks at such an angle that it took on wedge shape at the center of each. On each side of each step a crockery pot was placed upside down.

The sandy path bordered by tufts of wilted grass continued to yet another set of stairs on the opposite side of the house. This staircase wound around to the top of the deck on the upper second story. Its lower level served as a potting shed. The entire house even to the open roof gazebo, the ancient arbors and dilapidated gates consisted of unpainted cedar. Despite the cold, she could smell the aroma of cedar. She had every intention to go up one of the sets of steps. But at the last second she turned into the potting shed under the deck. Perhaps because she was distracted by the cracked strawberry jar filled with the remains of thyme, sage, oregano, yellow savory, gazania, allyssum and phlox. The remains consisted of dried up leaves stuck onto withered sticks. She broke off pieces and put them into an old handkerchief, she found in her pocket. She placed the handkerchief on the top of one of the potting tables.

On the wood tables were rows of neatly stacked clay pots. On the shelves under the tables were sacks of fertilizers, plant food, and garden tools. She knelt down resting her left knee on the brick and sand floor to lean as far back as she could reach to get a closer look at one of the sculpted terra cotta pots lining the far end of the shelf that rested against the crossed lattice woodwork nailed along the back of the potting shed. She stretched back to retrieve a particularly beautifully shaped clay pot when her bracelet fell off behind the shelf and in front of the crisscross lattice work. She tried for several very long minutes to retrieve her bracelet until finally her hand became stuck.

"Mrs. Longleaf is that you?"

"Ouch," she jumped and bumped her head on the underside of the potting table.

"I didn't mean to startle you. I just came home for lunch. Did you knock?"

"I'm afraid I'm stuck. No I didn't knock. That was my next step."

"My door is always unlocked. Just come in. Here let me help."

"I don't think I have a choice. I'm really stuck."

He knelt down beside her and reached to the back of the open shelf. He gingerly pulled the table out from the lattice wall. He took her hand with his and gently pulled her back into his lap. She did not resist. He opened her hand, pulled out a splinter with his fingers and kissed it. She was so intent on looking at his face, his features, and studying his demeanor, she did not pull away.

"You've got a scraped hand," he put her hand between his upper arm and his chest and gently pulled her toward him. She turned her face and he whispered into her ear.

She did not speak for a long minute. She was flattered. She could hear his heart beat. She was embarrassed.

"I have some questions for you."

"Did I turn in either of the reports? The answer to that is no," he looked down at her.

"Is this your house?" she was stalling.

"In about twenty-five years it will be. You've got a cob web in your hair," he said..

"You're right."

"About what in particular?"

"I may need your help. Can we be honest about one thing. We don't have to be honest about anything else. If I may determine the rules of engagement."

"Anything. Anything you want," he sighed.

Was he pleading?

"But I can't be sure of... of , as you say, anything right now," she was confused. What had she said to bring this type of response.

"I can tell you this. I found no reports from the Bay police. No missing person reports. You should not jog near that marina until ... until we figure out what is going on. Are we in agreement,?" He straightened her hair.

"But what about the past," she had made a slip. She had not intended to say anything, but to only ask questions. He threw her off with his confession that he had not turned in any report. She wondered why. Something was wrong somewhere. What had he spotted.

"What past. I'm too young to have a past. We're too new to have a past," he stopped when he heard her catch her breath.

"It's just us," he whispered. "Whatever we decide between us will only be between us. We don't need to share this with anyone. Do we? You decide."

"I'm not," Margaret sighed. She didn't want to hear his proposed pact.

"You're not ready?"

"That too. But more importantly, I'm not too young to have a past."

He made no response. He pulled her close to him. His hands warmed her back, her shoulders and back of her neck. The veins stood out on his neck. They were throbbing at his temples. She look at him at an angle to study this. She never closed her eyes.

"Will you promise to help me when I'm in a tight spot." She regretted making that request. In fact, she was beginning to regret the whole conversation. She panicked. She moved away, but then came back. He seemed to sense this conflict. They did not talk again for a long time. They were content to stay where they were while she came to a resolution. The sunlight streamed through the spaces between the deck boards above. She looked down onto his chest and then ran her finger along the line of light running diagonally across his black sweater. She could hear him breathing. A streak of light fell across his blond hair and down across his left gray eye and cheekbone to his neck. A lone mockingbird came to sit on the edge of the railing just above the lattice work. He flew off only after they again began to speak. Crows cawed incessantly from a nearby field.

"Yes, but only if you ask. I don't interfere. I won't ask questions if you don't want me to. Why?"

"I have a premonition," she reached up to run her fingers along the side of his face.

"A what?" he asked.

"Something they didn't teach in your criminology courses," she pulled away. She couldn't breath.

"Hey. Don't make fun of my age. Besides those were graduate courses. Strictly theoretical. I'm an aggie. Why were you crawling around the potting shed. Just out of curiosity," he kissed the right side of her face beginning at her cheekbone.

"I can't think right now," she said. "Interfere with what? I've got to go before," her voice trailed off.

He did nothing. He said nothing. They sat there in the potting shed waiting for her to continue to speak.

"But tell me what are your hours," she could not bring herself to admit to anything. It took everything out of her just to continue to compose and to ask a series of mundane questions.

He pulled took out a stick of gum, unwrapped it and put it in her mouth.

"Well this week I get off at three. Next week I go on at three. I'll write down the schedule and stick it on your backdoor."

"A penultimate question. Your gardens."

"I just cleaned up what was already here."

"And you've added to your garden... so says Alicia's mother," she made up the last comment.

"She's probably sitting at her window right now. The old lady likes to watch the leaves drop."

"I feel safe then," she laughed.

"You will always be safe with me."

It had begun to snow under the sunlight. There was no wind. The sound of the snow was like the sound of pine needles falling; sprit zing in bursts of light winds that swirled around outside in the silent gardens.

"What about the notice I found at Hank's."

"What notice."

"It's in my back pocket."

"I'll get it."

"Oh this," he pulled out and opened the BYOB notice. "I've sworn off beer," he crumpled up the notice with one hand and threw it onto the ground.

"Come in. Just for a minute to warm up. Your hands are cold. You're shivering."

"My cousin. She hired a PI. He'll be lurking about," she threatened.

"Tell me about this character. He'll stick out like a sore thumb around here," he spoke softly.

"You'd be surprised. He makes himself invisible. Anyway, Edna has hired him to find out what is going on and to act like some sort of bodyguard."

"Big sis. She thinks there's a problem."

"Yes. She's very protective. She just got herself a partnership in some little law firm up in Annapolis."

"The PI works for the law firm. Just out of curiosity how did she buy it?"

"Twenty year plan. It's like owning a mortgage."

"I'm sure she made a hefty down payment. And now what are you going to do?"

"I lent her some money too. What did you say?" she laughed.

"What kind of a partnership are you going to get into?"

"Well. I've been thinking about this very thing for some time. I really don't want anything too complex. Maybe a small real estate investment trust. Real estate investments are at their lowest level in years," She leaned back on her hands.

"I knew it."

"What did you know?"

"You're very competitive with your cousin,. Whatever your cousin wants or has, you've got to have. I'm very lucky. It all has to do with timing," he naively admitted.

Margaret blushed. How could he know something she could not admit even to herself. She let these remarks slide.

"Do you have water jurisdiction? I mean, for instance, can you arrest someone on the high seas?"

"Strictly county lands and the people and beasties that walk upon it." he said. "I went out to the marina because of your call. Technically, I don't have any jurisdiction."

She again made no move to protest. She saw no significance in his remark until sometime later. Until the incident yesterday, she had not known of his existence. He was telling her that he knew of hers.

"I found a piece of evidence."

"How critical would you say it is?"

"Very," she measured her words. She decided that she would share this information with him. What could he possibly gain by twisting any facts that she gave him. Since his jurisdiction was at issue, he was possibly an outsider too. In any case, he should provide a complete set of informational facts not just speculation to whomever would be assigned to this case.

"Why?"

"I am very certain it fell off of the corpse."

"Well? What would have fallen off a corpse. A hand. A head. A gun?"

"It's a shoe. A man's top sider."

"I can't say that it's critical. Why would you say it's critical?"

"I've got it at home. I think it's critical for two reasons. The first is of course, it was picked up at the crime scene."

"What is the crime scene?"

"The deck of the Saber. That item alone may help me prove that a crime actually took place. Also, it may very well prove that it belonged to the victim. Second and more importantly, we can possibly use it to identify the victim."

"You didn't mention this before. You actually climbed onto that Saber? That was a very dangerous thing to do. I say that not to alarm you, but to point out that when I arrived and when you return to the pier, the Saber was gone. I think that someone who was involved with whatever was going at the time was in the vicinity. Maybe you were not spotted, but maybe you were. You've got a lot of work cut out for you to do all of these things that you want to do."

"No. I didn't mention it before. I didn't...."

"Don't worry about it. You may start to remember other things."

"I remember describing the corpse has having on socks. Ugh. Its feet were bloated. No. Wait. There was something else. A very distinctive jacket. The maroon one with a Herron Bay crest."

He did not appear to recognize this significance of this statement.

"Will you give me some time to find out some of these things?"

"Time is short. I've got to turn over all of this information to county by the end of the day. That's procedure."

"Give me until tonight to come up with the proof I need."

"Maybe I can give you some slack. The best argument you can come up with is the corpse itself," he whispered.

She moved back toward him. The snow shower was over. Bit of the powdery snow fell through the deck above and onto them. The sun became warmer when the wind stopped.

"Tonight at the marina. Meet me about eleven. I will not be trespassing. I am a slip owner so I have every right to be in the marina compound anytime of day or night."

"Let me think about this. Come in. For just a minute. You've got to wash that hand. Its got a bad scrape."

"You've got city water don't you," she realized she had found a hidden treasure in this house. She wouldn't be forced to use her well water or to go up to the marina and light off the water heater and then wait forty-five minutes for it to warm up sufficiently to bathe.

"Sure do. Best water in this part of the county," he was tempting her. He stood up and pulled her up with him. "I've got a brand new hot water heater and a new water softener. You can't imagine how great the texture of the water is. It sure beats using the laundromat."

"Well maybe for a minute."

She unintentionally left behind her handkerchief filled with dried herbs.

CHAPTER 7

"Among other things I've come back to your shop to look at your Meissen pieces?"

"What is the occasion? You're dressed fit to kill."

Margaret laughed.

"Where's big Sis?"

"Up at the courthouse. Where else? Sometimes I think she lives there." Margaret took off her wool jacket. She had on a white silk blouse, charcoal gray slacks and black patent low heeled shoes.

"And...."

"She's researching your incorporation documents filed with the secretary of the state's office."

"The purpose...." He nervously pulled up the sleeves of his hunter green turtle neck. Today he appeared to be especially anxious.

"I can only guess. Make sure they were properly filed. She'll probably look for any outstanding liens? Though. I really don't know."

She followed him toward the north end of the shop through the maze of marble top tables, a Victorian settee newly upholstered in green silk print, sideboards, mirrored armoires, pie safes with intricately punched tin doors to the Henkle Harris corner cupboard. In this part of the shop the walls were filled with nineteenth century oil landscapes framed in gold plaster frames. The piece's hand rubbed mahogany surface shimmered under the light of the brass chandelier. Topped by a Federal style molded cornice, it dominated that whole section of the shop despite the fact it was partially hidden by a row of armoires. He had filled it with an assortment of porcelain tea pots, demi tasse sets of sixes or fours or pairs and singles and a full set of Lamoge. Silver spoons lined the front.

"What do you think of this soup tureen?" he opened the hand blown glass door. "I had this one at home."

"It's really magnificent," she took it down to examine the domed lid with an acorn shaped lid pull and to verify its markings.

"The crossed swords are xed out."

"That's because the artist who painted this tureen did not work for Meissen. The artist was independent and, in my opinion, more creative than the average run-of-the-mill Meissen artist."

"I'll be happy with just your run-of-the-mill."

She followed him into the office carrying the tureen. She almost tripped over the small space heater set upon the cement floor facing away from the door with its heating elements cracking. It provided the only light in that part of the room which consisted of a phosphorescent blur emitted from the set of bright red, glowing elements.

"I assumed that you are looking for nineteenth century." He looked up at her from the light under the desk lamp.

"Edna was precise. However, I'm going to need to see this porcelain in daylight. The light in here is no better than in the shop. Can I take it and bring it back tomorrow if I find any flaws?" She was trying to ignore the pallor that had settled across his face. He appeared even more gaunt then the day before. How could she have missed this. He appeared to be absolutely consumed with anxiety.

"I'm sure you won't find any flaws," he took the tureen, wrapped it in tissue paper and newspaper and put it in a cardboard box.

"And I would like to borrow your regatta jacket and this picture taken of the crew with the regatta cup. I will bring these back tomorrow with the check," she was standing by the wall covered with pictures. She walked over and took the jacket off of the Victorian coat rack and then walked back to carefully take down one of the pictures hung on the periphery of a large cluster pictures.

"Suit yourself my dear."

"Who is awarding the cup?"

"Let me see," he took the picture and placed it under the light. His hands were shaking slightly. He turned it over. "That's Harv Luttrell. We've written the names on the back. Let me see now...," he took out a stick of chewing gum. "I'm trying to give up smoking. Harv Luttrell. He had some kind of business dealings with Max over the years. He's known Max at least as long as he and, of course, Max. Max worked on the regatta committee. Why?"

"I think I'd like to talk to him. You know. To see if he any news at all about Maxim."

"Yes. Of course. Thanks for doing that. I guess Edna's too busy."

He took out his rolodex.

"Harv lives up on the West River. Here we are 16 Harbor Channel Drive. Take his business card."

"Before I go storming up there, you've got to do two things. First call him and have him meet me at Captain's Cove at…. Let's see it's six o'clock. Have him meet me at seven thirty. Tell him I'm a prospective business partner and you desperately need a reference. You must stress the urgency of this request. Let's see the urgency would be something like I am only offering this proposal to you for a short period of time."

He called the number and left a rambling message on Harv Luttrell's voice mail.

"I don't understand?" he whined as he hung up the phone.

"And second, fill me on with every bit of information that you can muster," Margaret was insistent that she finish her thought.

"The message that you just left is true, I am seriously thinking about investing in a business partnership. Maybe even yours," she pulled up a button tufted Victorian side chair to sit down on the other side of the light shaded in green glass to closely watch his face.

"I really don't know how I'm going to save this shop," he spoke softly. "After all of the years I put into it. I just can't seem to make it."

"As far as your business is concerned, I've been thinking and Edna's definitely been thinking. Between the two of us, we'll come up with something. Now let's talk about Maxim."

"What do you want to know? I keep all of my papers in this drawer," he pulled open a wooden desk drawer after jiggling it. The sides were cracked and stained black around the edges. It contained neatly arranged files. He pulled out one marked partnership agreement on the worn tab and handed it to her. She opened the folder and spread out all of the papers on the desk.

He got up.

"Sit here. I'm going to brew some tea," He turned on the hot plate element under a copper water kettle. At that moment someone came into the shop. Dan left the room to see if it was the individual he seemed to be expecting.

Margaret found several sets of photographs of the partners Max and Dan. Some dating as far back as fifteen years. They appeared to be taken on only special occasions: The opening of the shop, at a tenth anniversary celebration, someone's birthday. She recognized Max in the older pictures. She did not recognize him in the more recent ones. He had changed radically in appearance from a thin dark haired man to an overweight one, balding except for a gray fringe beginning at the temples with a full red beard. She was only able to recognize him in his more recent state because someone had written Max in ink over his chest in one of the very recent pictures as if to use it to identify him. She held this picture next to the regatta picture, but could not find him. Had his appearance changed again?

"Hi Dan. Has Max dropped by?" someone out in the shop asked.

Dan's voice was muffled.

"Haven't seen him lately. Anything I can do?"

"Yeah. We were expecting to meet with him this week." The sound of their conversation faded into the background as they moved away from the office door.

She picked up an onion skin letter. It was the color of saffron covered on the shiny side with sentences neatly printed in blue ink. The words were evenly spaced. It was dated 1971 and addressed to Dan. She skimmed over the formal opening and pleasantries to find buried in the central paragraphs and in the last paragraph of the letter a set of statements of what she considered to be an intention to form a co ownership of the shop. She set that aside to read through the formal partnership agreement. The partnership agreement itself was peculiar. It was not typed. It was handwritten. Its language was casually phrased in the everyday idiom. This particular effort was a radical approach to break away from normal business practices. She reasoned it must have been a direct result of the impact of the war upon the every day life even to the manner of transacting business. Formality in preparing official documents had all but disappeared as had the formality of even the shape of the business day itself when protests were scheduled during lunch hour only to last into the afternoons. Disruptions became an every day occurrence. She had forgotten how tumultuous those times had been.

"Where's Eustacia McSwiny?"

"Who?" Dan returned. He stood behind her looking over her shoulder for only a moment. He turned his attention to the noisy kettle. He picked up the lid of the china tea pot, poured in the hot water and then set in a silver tea leaf holder to steep.

"Maxim's first wife."

"I never met her. I never met any of his wives," he poured two cups of tea. Without asking set a cup of tea beside her with a sugar bowl filled with sugar cubes.

"Any of the kids?" she drank the tea after stirring in two cubes of sugar.

"The oldest kid. And the baby."

"I guess you'll be meeting them all by the time this er ah partnership matter is resolved." That last remark slipped by Margaret.

"I'm going to borrow three items. I'll make a note. Two pictures and the regatta jacket. Is this one yours? I guess everyone who crewed that regatta got one."

"Yeah. We each got one. I'll be right there," he called over his shoulder. He left the room with a flourish.

Margaret turned over the picture again to review the names. She knew only three. Distracted by the conversation taking place out in the shop, she put them into a manila envelope and went to the door of the office. Dan was speaking in a loud voice.

"I don't care about the tee three initiative."

"Tee plus," someone called.

"Whatever it is I won't settle those accounts in three days."

"Are you finished?"

"For now. Say who are those guys. This is the third time I've run into them in two days."

"If you're referring to George and Henry. They're friends of Max's. We used to like to invest by consensus. We considered ourselves as investors. They like to keep up with all of the latest market regulations. I don't give a rat's ass, if you will excuse the expression."

"If you're a trader...."

"No. No. As you can see for yourself," he pointed to a wall where he displayed his various licenses. As some sort of gesture, he encased the assortment of documents in antique frames. "I am a broker. Although I only work at it part time. Selling is like marketing. I love it. I also have a real estate license. What of it?"

"Just be careful. Volatile market these days. What about Maxim?"

"No. He was neither. But quite knowledgeable on the subject. He represented a few brokers in his day."

"Represent any recently?"

"At least two within recent memory. He lost both cases. Let's see," he drummed his fingers on the desk. "The most spectacular one was the Chapman case. I used to do research for him. On those two cases, I did some research. But I know he had someone else. One of the law clerks in his office. I don't think the kid was a good researcher, but Max wanted him to do the bulk of the work. I didn't complain when I found that all I had to do was to review the technics."

Margaret didn't answer.

"On the subject of a volatile market. It had to do with the failure to report the real value of stock on a particular set of financial statements. One set of quarterly financial statements in particular issued for one period of time. I think it was one of the broker-dealers who not only reported sold stock on the open market at market value, but also reported sold stock from an aging inventory at inflated prices. Or as they say above the true market value. Max lost on that one. Chapman had to pay heavy fines and penalties, and reimburse the plaintiff several hundred thousand dollars. The brokerage house could have lost a lot more. But Max, in my opinion, successfully showed that there is no market standard for reporting the so-called "true" value of stocks or bonds."

"I thought true was another word for historical. What its sales price was listed for in the financial section of the newspaper at some point."

"That's the argument he offered. The broker had used the historical value as sales price. He used the price of the stocks and bonds to value them at the time the firm purchased them, plus or minus an average value. With that argument Maxim caught the eye of the big syndicates."

"What is a big syndicate. And in what way."

"I'm talking international syndicates. One especially. Its headquarters is offshore. Probably run by Europeans. Anyway, I got the feeling that he made them very nervous. Stock ownership is used hereabouts as a measure of wealth."

"Strange, but true. A nasty habit that probably dates back to the Sumerians. But how do you know that he caught the interest of the syndicates."

"Correspondence he got. It certainly made the financial press. What Max did was pretty radical. You know," he paused. "He questioned an industry practice. The practice of valuation in the investments industry."

"You mean an expectation that a potential investor would expect to find in a set of financial statements. An expectation to be used for credit purposes. I mean like for acquiring a liquid asset like money from stockholders?"

"In a word. Yes," he whispered and then turned to yell. "I'm coming."

"Where is the correspondence that you referred to?"

"I kept only one letter. It's in one of those cubby holes. Look for yourself," he left the room.

"Maxim. Oh Maxim. You radical. What have you done?" she poured herself another cup of tea. She stood up to look through the cubby holes lined along the back of the desk and just under the curve of the roll top. She found a tissue paper thin envelope with a Bermuda stamp postmarked Hamilton on it. The return address consisted of a foreign sounding business ending in the "Ltd" abbreviation. She took it and put it in her purse along with the photographs.

Dan again returned to find Margaret finishing the last of her tea.

The phone rang. Dan answered. He spoke only three words.

"You're on. Harv will meet you at Pirates Cove."

"I'm on my way. I have only one question. Why am I wearing the regatta jacket."

"What do you expect to find?"

"I really have a set of expectations. I think he is a critical piece to this puzzle surrounding Maxim."

"Heaven forbid that I should have any information that's of use to anyone."

"Dan. Don't you see it? It all has to do with the regatta. I know it."

"How about this. You're Max's latest."

* * *

Margaret found the restaurant almost empty. She was able to pick the table she wanted and sat facing the marina. Even in the winter darkness lit only by a few pier lights, Margaret lingered over the view of the yachts lined up in slips spreading down pier where out beyond the last yacht, the last marina, the West and South rivers met. The only people in the restaurant were those who lived nearby. During the sailing season, the place was usually filled with yachtsmen motoring up and down the intercostals, who had decided to stay overnight at the cinderblock yacht motel.

She was seated in a white wicker chair at a table covered with pink linen table clothes and napkins wrapped tightly and placed in wine goblets. A party of eight drifted in to sit at a long table facing the West River in the opposite end of the restaurant. She hid behind a large leather bound menu book. Harv Luttrell did not show for another twenty minutes. He had apparently been sitting at the bar. When he did appear, he had difficulty speaking. He was carrying a drink with him. Margaret assumed that he was sloshed.

"So. My dear. You're thinking of investing in the antique business. You are better advised in investing your money elsewhere."

"I have my heart set on it. Tell me," she picked up a glass filled with soda and lime. "How did you find Dan and Maxim."

"A very unlikely pair."

"Business wise."

"Conservative. Yes. That's the word I'd use to describe how they conducted their business. Take the Water Tort for example. Maxim made his payments on time. In fact, I think she's paid off. What more can you ask?"

"Thank you for that nice reference. Can I have a business card?"

He handed her one that he kept in a gold tone business card case. She wrote on the back of the card with her pen. She turned the card over and looked at it for a long minute.

"I'll be back in a minute," she got up deliberately to show off the regatta jacket. She went to the ladies room and returned a short time later to be followed to her table by the waitress.

She sat.

"I think I'll have the trout stuffed with crab meat."

"I'll have a blue steak medium," he gave Margaret a side long glance. "What is that you have on my dear. It looks very familiar."

"I should hope so. Don't you have one?"

"Yes. Whose is that?"

"It's Maxim's."

He started.

"Just out of curiosity. Did you know Eustacia?" she was waiting for him to recover.

"Who?"

Margaret didn't reply immediately. They were distracted by the table of eight. A gray haired man with young features dressed in a navy blue sports jacket and white Izod knit shirt got up and came over to their table.

"Hi Harv. I see you've got part of your crew with you."

"Oh Sam. For goodness sake. It's you. I'd like you to meet Margaret Longleaf. Sam Morton heads up the Regatta Committee. Is that who's sitting at the long table?"

"Yep. We' holding a spring regatta this year. First weekend in May. What do you think of fifty dollars as an entrance fee?"

"Fair fee. What will be the qualifications?"

"We're just going by boat size. We'll start with the twenty footers. Maybe seventeen. Depends."

"Who will be your observers?"

"Mark and Cal. As usual. They're sitting on the end." Margaret turned to look at them.

"The first week end in May," he took out his pocket calendar. "I'll mark the calendar. Sam let me have your phone number again. I've misplaced it."

"Call me at the Ship Chandler's Inn. Here take my card. And thanks Harv. Nice meeting you Mrs. Longleaf."

"You won't join us?"

"No. Thank you. The meeting is just getting started. We're looking for volunteers," he left as the waitress approached the table to serve dinner.

"Maybe we'll join you for dessert," Margaret called.

"I like volunteering Mr. Luttrell," she whispered.

"Please call me Harv. What did you order?"

"Sea trout stuffed with crab meat. It is very delicate in flavor."

"I ordered blue. It's a bit heavy."

"As I've always said thank goodness for people like you."

"What does that mean."

"You will eat up all of the blues," she announced triumphantly.

"You do have to acquire a taste for it. I must admit. Now who were you asking about?"

"Eustacia McSwiny. Maxim's wife."

"That's not the name of his ex wife. It's Lenore or something like that."

"She was his first wife. We went to school together."

"My goodness. You go back a long way. Come to think of it. His first wife is dead. This happened very recently. A year or so ago. I could be wrong," he took his napkin and wiped the corners of his mouth. He wore a crested ring on his pinkie.

"I'll have go back through my alumni newsletters. You know I didn't really realize who Maxim's was. He has changed so in appearance. Take a look at this photo would you. That is Maxim isn't it?"

"It's Max all right. See I'm presenting the cup to the Danny and Max. Cal Thompson and Mark Perry are standing behind me. And behind the boys is a very devious sort. Sir Josiah Chatswith. I think that's his name. Ugly man."

Margaret took a long look at the photo. The man he was pointing to was a sharp featured man, blond complected wearing European black rimmed glasses, an ascot, dark jacket with gold monogrammed buttons and captain's hat.

"A title? He looks British."

"He might be. Or maybe South African. Probably from Maida Vale. He's an arms dealer for the Birmingham syndicate among other occupations."

"By using the descriptive term ugly do you mean tough to deal with?"

"Very difficult individual. He won't take no for an answer. Wanted to buy Dockers's marina. Offered a fabulous price for it. When Cas. He's sitting with the group over there. When Cas Hoeff turned him down, he got really nasty. He got into the group through Max. Max...."

"Max had probably done some work for him."

"Could be. He works out of his yacht off of Point No Point. That is when he's in our waters."

"Maxin has an office on a yacht?"

"No. Sir Josiah."

"Is that his boat?" she pointed to a boat in the background.

"No. That's not the Josiah."

"Bad omen to name a boat after yourself."

"He's a bad omen period. He owed Max some money or Max owed him some money. Let me tell you something about Max. The minute that guy appeared on the scene. Max changed. I have never seen anyone change so. I had Max on retainer for years. He handled all of our legal problems. We used to have dinner once a month."

"Yes. I've got to talk to Max."

"You should before you invest in the shop. Haven't seen him in a couple of months. The last time I saw him to talk to him was in December. Or did we have lunch in January? He called to say he was going to send over another proposal from that Josiah character. He knew how I felt about the man. Yet he persisted in putting together proposal sets and faxing them to my office."

"What didn't you like about them?"

Margaret put the photo back into her purse and ate quickly. She slowed down only to savor the sautéed zucchini, yellow squash and spring onions flavored with basil. She drank only tap and sparkling water with her meal.

"Well, for one important reason. Maxim was to put together a group of investors headed up by Sir Chatswith. The investors were to put up about ninety percent of the money. Chatswith was not only to head up the investors, but he was also to manage the group's resources. In other words, he was to hold the money."

"He would most likely take the money out of the country."

"Not good. I don't think a local bonding company would touch a nonresident alien. For the simple reason that they can not really do an adequate credit check locally."

After Harvey Luttrell finished the cocktail, he ordered a cabernet sauvignon. At his insistence, he gave her half a glass of wine. Under duress Margaret accepted, but used the first sip to toast Max. She made a deliberate effort not to finish the glass of wine despite the fact that it followed her from table to table.

"To my new adventure. Turry Top Antiques."

"Here. Here. To your adventure. You will be successful provided you buy out Max's share. He has only one interest now. The Brigamton syndicate. As strange as this may sound, its his all consuming passion. I'm running a full corporate check on that syndicate," he sipped his drink between thoughts.

"Brigamton syndicate? Is that the same as Brigamton Firearms."

"I think the syndicate bought the rights to use the name," he inhaled. "That happened several years before the rebellion."

"Which one?"

"The only one I know of in the land of Hibernia my dear. A corporation will take on the personality of its managers. From what I can gather, a small guerrilla company was started maybe five years ago by this Sir Josiah. He was brought into a small paper producing unit to look at the cost of processing the product and marketing it. He was so successful in raising the profit level that the old and very ancient management culture just sold that piece of the company for a small amount with a percentage return on the profits for five or ten years. He used that as his seed money. He does have a philosophy. Although I've not yet figured it out."

"Are you telling me of some kind of a connection between the ongoing rebellion and the syndicate?"

"I suspect so. Piracy, gun running might not be the worst of it."

"Radical. Then buying out Max is a very good idea, but...."

"Buy him out. I urge you. Money is no problem. I'll put together something."

"It's more than that. Dan and I can't seem to find him. In fact, Dan has not seen him in a couple of months."

"You haven't seen him lately?"

Margaret deliberately did not answer or even acknowledge this question. She noticed that a pallor had begun to settle over his face. She realized that Max's absence had upset him even before he admitted it to himself.

"Well neither have I. Yes. He has been acting strangely for the past few months. He should be here tonight with the regatta committee. Be sure they will want to know why he is missing or where he's got to. Most likely you'll find him with Josiah. I tell you that man is all consuming. Max is like his pawn. Max is like a different person. It's hard to describe this difference not only in his behavior, but also in his demeanor," he anticipated her next question. "I'd go so far to say that the man broke up Max's marriage. Simply because he detested Lenore. I think that's her name. A young foolish woman."

They were interrupted by a man who looked to be in his late thirties wearing an Irish knit sweater over kaki's. He was immediately recognized.

"Well hello Cas. I would like you to meet Margaret Longleaf."

"Come along and join us for dessert. Hello Margaret. Come and sit next to my wife Martene. She's one bored cookie. But before we order. Harv we've got to talk. Just for a minute," he guided Margaret over to the long table, made the introductions, seated her next to a young woman who looked to be in her late twenties and took Harv out to the dock. Margaret was able to strategically position herself so that she did not lose the view.

"Wind has come up," Margaret said to the young woman after ordering lemon apricot cheesecake.

Out on the dock, framed in a series of bay windows lining the east wall of the restaurant, they could see the halyards flapping incessantly under the string of lights along the pier. Harv took out his pipe and had begun to smoke it. He folded his left arm as if to hold up his right arm, using his right hand to signal the importance of the points he was making.

CHAPTER 3

Margaret returned to find the house was without light, but not foreboding. The electricity must have gone off again she reasoned. When this occurred, the automatic light timer attached to the lamp on the serving cupboard in the dining room was no longer in sync to turn on at four thirty pm and to turn off at one thirty am.

A typical mid Atlantic colonial, the house sat under knarled oaks whose discarded leaves floated back and forth in the wind gusts along bay front forming lacy pools that would disappear almost as soon as they took shape. The wood structure was framed in white, almost a pearl white, that appeared luminescent almost glowing even under the weakest moon light. Passing clouds cast only temporary dark shadows as they floated north toward the bay bridge. Sounds burst in and then dissipated making it hard to tell whether the creaking noises came from the house itself moving in the wind off of the bay or from the branches high above. Tiny moving lights flickered from a passing cargo ship out in the ship's channel on its way to the port of Baltimore. Stationary lights blinked erratically from Comyns Islands nestled off the eastern shore on the eastern side of the bay.

Margaret opened the glass casement door to find the house was warm and to find Chester waiting impatiently just inside the doorway. He was sitting beside the forced air vent. His tail thumped against the square tube housing the forced air duct. The thumping made a hollow sound echoing under the house.

Out of habit, he gulped into his lungs a series of long drafts of the night air. Despite the wet cold air causing him to sneeze, he ran past her down the steps across the lawn into the darkness. Without a moment's hesitation, he trotted up the heavily rutted gravel alley in a dancing gate. This journey was to be marked with a series of distractions first to chase fox and deer under the waning moon. On that particular night, the landscape was full of shimmering standing pools covered with the thinnest layer of ice. They had formed in clusters along the roadside and beyond the wood nearest the encircling wetlands.

The night air was thick with humidity. Spots of frost began to form sticking to the top of his head and down his back. He stopped to lick the ice. Under the weight of his frame, his paws broke through the edge of the pool. Water jets shot up through the broken ice as he put pressure on the top layer of ice. Leaves coated with slime lining the bottom of the pool stuck to his paws. He shook his head at the sight of himself reflecting up from a mosaic of ice and leaves under the light attached to the electric pole overhead. A row of these poles was planted every fifty or a hundred feet along the alley. Soaked in creosote, each pole was characteristically scarred with chinks of splinters and rows of iron hooks. Occasionally one would fall across the roadway. This would occur usually after a very wet storm.

Steam rolled out of his nostrils and up into the air. He held his nose up into the air to catch any unusual scent. He caught one. The leaves fell away from his paws as he again proceeded to trot down the gravel lined ally to investigate the sounds made by a pair of raccoons scavenging near Johnson's garage several blocks down toward town.

He spotted a lone fox out of its den to hunt fleecy coated mice, who lived in neatly stacked wood piles near the trash cans lining the alley. The bushy fox pounced upon a mouse eating leftover chicken. He caught the mouse off guard and scooped it up to return to his den.

Chester took chase. He pursued the fox across the thicket of heaving earth covered with prickly brush to the wood across the meandering road lined with ditches. The fox dived into a series of parallel mounds of leaves that looked like the Spottsy earthworks. After he was well into the wood, Chester unexpectedly sunk down into the leaves. He yipped with surprise. The echo made him stop to listen for other sounds. Spindly trunks of oak and maple and sumac jutted up into the night sky and moved ever so slightly despite the thundering bay winds roaring in spurts overhead. The fox scurried over a fallen log and jumped into a gully between one of the mounds of leaves before crossing the back road and disappearing from sight. With great difficulty - almost as if treading water, he turned about face and headed back toward the roadside.

A spindly fawn stood awkwardly on the brow of the road. It appeared to be dazed. It shivered. Its head drooped. Its tiny hooves made clicking sounds as it moved along the roadbed. Chester approached cautiously. It stopped to turn and look at him before resuming its run. It sensed that he was not a threat, and decided to clatter at a leisurely pace down the double line in the center of the road. Chester whimpered and followed cautiously eyeing its sharp, but dainty hooves. His experience with horses boarded in the old hay barn taught him to be wary of the hooves, no matter the size, and to remain at a specifically measured distance in case of surprise movements. A silent gust of wind came up from the wetlands bringing with it a snow shower despite moon beams sticking out through holes in the overhanging, but swiftly moving clouds and despite the bitter cold night hovering the clouds hung suspended between the moon and the wood below.

An unexpected fast moving set of squalls came up from the mouth of the bay, one hundred or so miles due south east. It contained snow and pelting ice showers that moved in a string of diagonal lines blanketing the shore line under cover of thick low hanging cumulus. This squall caused a temporary white out. When the last squall passed inland, it moved quickly and left an eerie illuminated darkness.

Off shore flocks of migrating ducks and geese floated easily upon the south moving currents. Flocks of migrant water fowl covered the water as far as the eye could see in the years before the great eradication. The flocks now covered no more than a quarter mile of water surface at any one time. This night of erratic winds and squalls would hasten their journey southward. Some put their heads under their wings as ice pellets hit and bounced into the water: Most would not.

The moving figures on the nightscape now included a hunter prowling along the fringe of the wetlands. He docked the camouflaged barge at the commercial pier jutting out from Wineman's inlet in anticipation of the early morning duck shoot. Such barges, covered with evergreen branches, were allowed on the bay only during hunting season. The hunting permits, duck stamps, allowed each barge to follow the flocks at a specified distance. Each had an outboard motor and, on any day during hunting season, could be seen driving up and down through the two foot chop not far behind flocks of resting but jittery fowl.

Uninformed, he was hunting quail nests under moonlight. The sudden darkness sent him up the road to the marina into the island. The barge now far behind him rocked violently on the outgoing tide. In the ensuing line of squalls, unanchored and not securely moored at the dock, the barge would become loose in the winds. Caught in an unexpected, but swiftly moving tide, it would bounce back and forth along the perimeter of the rocky bulkheads lining the entrance channel to the bay and float out into the shipping channel to drift aimlessly in the black waters of the bay.

As suddenly as it happened it was over. Shots rang out with accompanying bursts of light that in reality did not occur simultaneously, but in succession only after several required mechanical actions. These spurts lasted only a millisecond in an undefined period of time like some misshappened star exploding in a series of bursts out beyond the atmosphere. The sounds did not echo. Under the temporary, but heavy cumulus, the gun shots sounded like a series of thuds.

* * *

Margaret changed into nubby long johns she found in the bottom drawer of the dresser in the cold back bedroom, rinsed the lotion off of her face with tap water, brushed her teeth with bottled water, and then sat under the light in the most uncomfortable chair in the living room in order to read. Sounds from the winds floated into the long room from the enclosed fireplace. The light in the living room flickered. She began with a copy of the county newspaper she found stuffed in the mailbox. The local news consisted of tedious descriptions of newly constructed additions to the shopping mall outside the nearest Arundel township on route four. The interview with the manager of a local car dealership consisted of five paragraphs on the location and its size. She glanced through the penny saver paper, always disappointed for some unspecific reason, and then fell asleep.

She awoke to the familiar popping sound. She walked out to look at the Sears wall clock hanging in the dining room. It was eleven. The clock began to chime. The sound of the chimes was tinny in resonance and each individual chime was short in duration. She opened the blinds to look out to find snow cover. It had stopped snowing some time earlier.

She dressed in navy sweat pants, ski jacket and boots. After searching for a short period of time, she found a flash light in the lower drawer of the buffet on top of a stack of neatly folded table linens.

She took keys from her purse, put on a knit hat and lined gloves and left to begin the search for Chester.

Since the layer of snow had been thinly dispersed, it did not hinder travel. Thus, the walk up the alley was not difficult. Her boots crunched down into the gravel. She whistled. This sound startled a nest of barn swallows roosting in the rafters of Pittman's garage. They made rustling sounds and then went back to settle into the bottoms of their mossy nests. She continued to follow the rutted alley only to turn to walk up one of the long drives to the road to the marina. By the time she reached the road, she spotted a county cruiser sitting in idle and waiting up by her lane.

"Jim. I'm glad to see you. It's Chester. He went out and has not come back."

"I thought I saw you. How long have you been out here? Come on and get in. We'll find him."

"Did you hear a popping sound about twenty minutes ago?"

"No," he looked at his watch. "No I didn't. I was down in South Neck."

He backed the car into the lane and turned it around.

"I thought I saw something down this way." He drove slowly back down the road for about a mile.

"There it is," he pulled into another of the long line of drives running perpendicular to the road and parked. He did not turn off the engine. He left it running in idle. He got out and walked back to the road.

Margaret followed him. Circles of light from the flashlights were moved methodically back and forth across the drive and then across the road. A dry easterly wind had come up. Loose snow swirled in a circular motion along the road surface and then up off the ground for short periods of time. These wind gusts created a stylized pattern in the snow along the uneven road surface.

"See those dark spots. I think it's blood," he pointed to spots of dark melting snow.

They walked for some minutes over terrain that was littered with clumps of brush, tree limbs, broken tree trunks and decaying logs. The ground was spongy and covered with layers of leaves dusted in spots with powdery snow. They did not speak again until they found Chester.

He was awake and lying close to the tiny feet of the doe on the wetlands side of a ten foot log. His head rested on his front paw. It was as if some great chase had taken place and Chester and the doe had come to rest in a hollowed out place for a moment in the quiet of the night. The moon came out sporadically between passing clouds. Its light moved in streaks across the landscape. Margaret so engulfed with Chester that at first took no notice of the doe. Sporadic light from the passing moon light shown upon its milky tan hairs now glistening from the light powdery snow cover. Its eyes were frozen open in a last gaze. No marks distorted its shape. It had fallen on the side disfigured from buckshot. Delicate ribs encasing its frame shown as gentle ripples under the newly grown winter coat.

"I'll go get a blanket. It'll just take a minute. Don't worry."

Chester made no attempt to get to his feet. He whimpered sporadically. Margaret knelt to comfort him. She ran her hand over his head and stomach, down his back and up his throat in separate movements. She warmed his paws with her hands. They were wet. It was then he yipped at her touch.

Jim wrapped a piece of flimsy plastic around him and then covered him with a blanket before picking him up. Both he and Margaret had difficulty carrying him away from the doe. Chester was able to squirm for only a minute before giving in to the pain. Jim carried him to the car and placed him on the back seat. Margaret remained only to cover the doe with a thin layer of leaves as if the cover of leaves would bring about a warmth. It was a fruitless gesture.

"I know the vet in Huntingdown. It won't take us any time to get there," he called the vet's office using the police dispatch phone.

"Of all places to have to go on a night like this," she mused aloud.

During the twenty minute trip, the warm air from the car heater gradually expanded to reach them in the backseat, but not until they reached the upper end of route two/four. Both Chester and Margaret fell asleep until the car turned sharply off the highway and jolted over the back road filled with gravel to the vet's office, a small room off the parlor on the first floor of a farmhouse.

The gingerbread house was top heavy with three turrets outfitted with rounded wooden shakes and trimmed in ornate moldings. It sat on a hill surrounded by overgrown fields. A stand of evergreen trees had been planted at the north end of a sloping front yard. They were placed there to act as a buffer against the northerlies. Beyond it due west stood a windmill and beyond that a tobacco barn, closed up for the winter, and a larger barn used to house livestock. These barns and several other outbuildings were painted dark red with white trim. Spotlights screwed into the corners of these buildings were turned on. With the exception of adding indoor plumbing and electricity, it looked as if the house was last remodeled during the Victorian era.

* * *

Despite his small size and advanced age, the veterinarian carried Chester to a large stainless steel sink. The floor was covered with linoleum and was spotless. He was bathed and then wiped dry with a terry cloth towel, examined, and stitched Chester, who had suddenly turned cantankerous.

"Let's clean up this bad boy," he said.

"Got a little piece of buckshot in him all right. Bring that light over here. Will ya Jim? He's lucky boy. Jim you hold his belly. Hands on either side. Young lady, you hold his head."

Margaret held him, but kept her eyes shut.

They stood in the center of a room painted gloss white with nothing in it except for a stainless steel sink and table. Overhead a fluorescent light fixture hung from white tubes extending down from the ceiling.

"This time of year you've got to keep the dogs inside. Hunters will shoot at anything that moves. Cows, sheep, themselves even. Never seen anything like it until recently. They're out there twenty-four hours a day. Why just last year one of Beall's horses was shot. That ended his career as a show horse."

"Was he disfigured?"

"Nope. Just addled."

"What's that?"

"Horse and people can become addled. It happens usually after a bad experience or an accident of some kind. They have a difficult time adjusting to their new circumstance. Horses become addled very easily. Horses, especially show horses tend to be neurotic. High strung. Too much inbreeding I've always said. Ever notice how they get a neurotic tick if you treat 'em too mean or even if you don't pamper 'em. This leads to poor performance. Such as stopping short of a jump for no good reason. Throwing out a shoulder after a few practice jumps. Beall regularly hires a chiropractor to come a put his prize show horses' shoulders back into their sockets."

"A what?"

"A chiropractor actually has to come out, strap the horse to the side of the stall and pull the horse's shoulder out to realign it. He then got to push it back into the socket. Takes two people usually. Usually not painful to the horse."

"How about Chester? Has this trauma addled him?"

"Chester? What do you mean? This fine specimen of a Lab."

"Will he be addled?"

He did not answer for several minutes.

"More than likely. Chester has had a trauma all right," he held Chester's head in both of his hands and looked into his eyes. "But more importantly he'll limp for a while," he pushed his wire rimmed glasses to the top of his head.

"Buckshot hit the bone?"

"No. No. The bone was missed. He got a hit in the groin though. He's going to be tender. Bring him back in a couple of days. I'll take out the stitches," he chewed his words.

Despite the late hour, he was dressed in a neatly creased pair of kaikis and blue levi shirt under his white medical overcoat.

"See here," he turned Chester over on his back to point to the location of the stitches. He looked at Margaret. "A little squeamish are ya. I'm going to put a paper collar on him so he doesn't lick the stitches. The collar is just temporary."

"By the way. That'll be forty-five."

Jim handed him two twenties and a five. He carried his wallet in his back pocket. The vet left the room to go into the parlor. Margaret watched him head toward a pine sink and turn on a converted oil lamp. It had a red glass shade. He took out a receipt book from a shelf underneath, tore out a slip perforated at one end, dated and signed it with a fountain pen he kept in an ink well. He returned to the office to give the receipt to Margaret. She put it in the pocket of her ski jacket.

"For services rendered," he winked at Jim.

* * *

"I'm going off duty. It has been quiet this evening. Except for Chester."

"What?"

"My tour is over."

"Oh. Yes," she thought for a long moment. "Why don't you come in for some coffee."

He did not answer for some minutes.

"We'll go to my place I think you're safer there. We'll go up and look at the house in daylight. It's just a temporary measure."

"What did you see?"

"Maybe I didn't see anything of significance. I can't be sure. However, a set of lights down on bay front. Could have been from out on the pier."

"Was it a boat?"

"I didn't have a chance to go up the alley before you whistled."

"I'm sorry. Why didn't you take a closer look?"

"You whistled."

"Did I whistle? In the middle of the night. Oh. Yes. Of course. I was whistling for Chester. I just do it out of habit I guess. What would Granny say."

"What?"

"You know the old expression -- a whistling girl and crowing hen are sure to come to some bad end."

"What are you not telling me Margaret," he turned off of route two-four and pulled immediately into the new parking lot butting against the 18th century cemetery. He left the engine running, but turned off the lights. The colonial church rebuilt early 19th century sat on a knoll above them and the cemetery.

"Lots."

"For now I'm talking about this murder that you reported," he sighed.

"Oh that," she moved across the plastic bench seat. "As a matter of interest, we've split up the search for the victim -- possible victim -- into two separate projects. We have to decide whether or not he is dead or has disappeared now for two reasons."

"They are...."

"His estate. He owned part interest in several businesses. And he had some people he was supporting and, if dead, heirs to his estate. One of his business partners hired Edna to represent his interest in the partnership."

"Is that project number one?"

"Yes. Project number two really has to do with who he was involved with recently that caused either his death or his disappearance. We're considering that whole issue as an adjunct."

"You and big sis are going around asking questions," he interrupted and pulled her closer.

"Yes."

"Have you thought about some of the dangers out there?"

"Something is out there all right," she shivered. "I can't quite be sure exactly what it is. It may be nothing."

He pulled her to his chest and kissed her cheekbone. She did not resist. Chester growled from the back seat.

"You smell like smoke."

"Everyone in the restaurant smoked."

"What?"

"Pirate's Inlet. I went up to meet the regatta committee."

"You are on that committee?"

"Oh, no. I could be on the committee though if I wanted. I wasn't an intruder. The only requirement they can enforce is renting a slip in the marina. It's easy to check. I'm on the list of renters. I was asking questions about Maxim."

"They are high profile," he whistled. "They own some politicians."

"They certainly are an unassuming group of people."

"Don't be fooled by appearances. Now who exactly is this Maxim?" he looked out toward the cemetery. "Did you see the white owl? That's a good omen," he stiffened.

"Where?"

They did not speak for a long time.

"He nests up in the bell tower and is rarely seen," he whispered.

"Who is Maxim?" he turned to face her in the darkness.

"There he is sitting on the tombstone,"

* * *

Margaret awoke to what appeared to be early morning gray mist. She heard Chester at the foot of the bed. He was whining and chewing his tongue. The spool bed creaked as she got up to throw off the wedding pattern quilt. It had a lumpy mattress of heavy batting dimpled by large shell buttons sewn into the ticking at regular intervals. The mattress rested on hemp configured in a jacob's ladder pattern. The white cotton sheet covering the mattress had pulled off at one corner. The wide pine boards were warm under her feet. Despite the attempt to finely sand the old wood planks, brown knots stuck up here and there. On impulse, she crawled under the bed to look at the inside of the finely turned legs. Chester followed.

She lead him downstairs to the back door set in an entry way located off of the kitchen to let him wander outside in the skeletal remains of the back garden now enshrouded in rolls of mist. The house was empty.

After reading a note she found stuck to the refrigerator door with a plastic magnet, she drank a glass of orange juice from a pitcher she found in the refrigerator and toasted two pieces of wheat bread, which she then covered with margarine and blackberry jam. She then toasted two more pieces of bread. She ran back upstairs so that she could take a coveted shower in a back bedroom she found that had been converted into a bath. Its walls were painted a flat snow white with a border of steamships, skipjacks and such. The triangular shower stall had rounded edges, encased in glass polymer and was set upon a floor covered with white and black mosaic tile. A small oak dresser bowed in the front with ornate brass knobs stuck to the front of each drawer was placed next to the pedestal sink and under a window overlooking the back porch. The woodwork was stained, not painted. The only mirror in the bath was a ten by ten encased in a maple frame attached to a shaving stand centered on the oak dresser. She found a towel and wash cloth in one of its top drawers.

Margaret dried herself in the warmth of the cast iron radiators hidden below the billowing steam. The clouds of steam were temporarily suspended in the trapped air and held in the confines of the room. Without warning, she felt a sudden draft upon her back. The escaping vapor dissipated clinging only to the mirror. Chester had pushed open the door. He pranced across the floor. He looked like a Jacobite in his white collar. He came up to her to lick her feet. She nudged him away with her ankle. He withdrew to sit next to the radiator.

"How did you get in?"

She turned to find Jim standing beyond the doorway framed with a dark pine molding.

"You left the door unlocked." he said.

"Why is it? You make me forget my age," she laughed.

CHAPTER 9

"Listen to me. Listen." Margaret held the phone out from her ear. "I've been up all night with Chester. Had to take him to the vet. He was shot. Why was he shot? Got me. Just teasing. Edna I was just teasing you. Yes. As in teasing. However, I don't think it was deliberate," she winked at Jim. "OK. OK. I'll meet you in forty-five minutes. Yes I know the place, but give me the address. What is the address! Nuts. I've got to drive across the bridge" she wrote down the address on a notepad she found on top of the desk.

A seasonal morning mist had just begun to dissipate from the surface of the bay. Sunlight changed from dim streaks of light to glaring shafts.

"I am going to run an errand," Margaret said over her shoulder as she climbed the stairs. "I'll have to take Chester with me unless...."

"I can come back in an hour or so to let him out."

"Thank you," she called from the top of the stair. She had at some later point decided to take Chester with her.

* * *

"I've always liked eating in the old manse."

"As for me," Margaret frowned. "What's up?"

"Eustacia."

"Who?"

"Who? What?" Edna mimicked Margaret. "Eustacia McSwiney."

"Maxim's Eustacia?"

Edna looked down at the sheaf of papers in front of her.

"But she's dead. It was printed in the alumni news."

"We found her," Edna pulled out a newspaper clipping with a name and address neatly typed below the clipping.

"Where and why," Margaret wondered out loud as she studied the clipping.

"Due east on the Wye. You get to go see her."

"When?"

"Now. I've brought a map. We have to strike...."

"Please no colloquialisms. Can I eat lunch first? Your treat?"

"You're the class rep. Catch my drift."

"Ugh. Of all things to be. Well, I guess it's my turn."

"Your turn."

"To play games."

"And I thought this was going to be a boring lunch. Tell me. Tell me."

"Don't you remember Constance Gantly?"

"Their money was in coal."

"Yes. They owned a wheel works depot in southwest."

"Are you sure."

"The original building was located on Spring street near the mouth of Tiber creek. Now why does the name of that street ring a bell. I don't think the street or at least that end of it exists any longer. The old cobblestones started at the river when there was a commercial port or was it just a quay on the river. Anyway, the old depot was located next to the train tracks. Spring street I'm certain. Have you ever eaten in that little restaurant down on Market? What ambiance. It will give you a flavor of the neighborhood: Back in the good old days when trains took over shipping coal from the canal barges. That family owned a fleet of coal trucks. Used of course to make local deliveries. In the days before oil when those sleek electric street cars zipped quietly around the city," she paused.

"This has nothing to do with anything. But there was a scandal in Constance's family. An older sister's boyfriend shot himself playing Russian roulette. Constance and those sisters. They all had red hair. Or they may have been her cousins."

Edna's eyes lit up. She put down the folder and picked up the menu.

"You remember everything," she coaxed.

"Constance forever the vindictive, spiteful, manipulative she wolf. Those are the kinds of things that I can talk about with Eustacia. Just idle chatter. However, to get information out of her is another matter. For one thing, she may not know or worse she may not remember."

"You've got enough ammunition to trigger something."

"Let's just say this. I've got enough to start a friendly conversation. Before we pursue this any further, I'd better call her," Margaret stood up looking around the restaurant for a phone.

"I already called her," Edna said from behind the menu.

Before Margaret could respond, a flustered waiter stopped only long enough to take their lunch order before rushing off in the general direction of the kitchen. She sat down to order a bowl of she crab soup, a small nicoise salad and a glass of Prince Michael. Her deliberate manner added further to his frustration.

They drank water from heavy pressed glass goblets and they buttered their rolls on pewter plates stamped with the image of George Washington's head under the phrase independence and Washington encircling it. They sat under wall paper of hunting scenes. Edna would occasionally comment on the one she favored just over Margaret's left shoulder. It depicted master of the hounds on horseback surrounded by hunters. All stood above a pack of beagles painted in pale browns, beige's, and creams. Their assorted poses gave one the impression that they were ready to follow the hunt master.

"Did you notice that?"

Edna didn't answer. She was sorting the papers in the manila folder.

"The waiter didn't write anything down."

"Didn't take the menus either," she put them on the empty chair. She pulled the folder out from underneath and put it on top. It was marked the Lazarus file.

* * *

"It was certainly nice of you to let me visit and on such short notice," Margaret spoke all the pleasantries.

"Why you just don't know what a delight," Eustacia directed Margaret to a chair, sat her in the chair, and turned on the lamp. As she bent down to turn on the lamp, she came close to take a brief look.

Margaret looked up an smiled. The light from the lamp shown on her face from underneath highlighting not only her features, but also the texture of her skin.

"Margaret I don't think you've changed a bit since school." She was wearing a pair of faded kakis, a yellow button down shirt with a crest embroidered on its pocket, and blue leather wooden shoes. The leather was attached to the wooden shoes with upholstery tacks.

"Thank you. I think I could sit here all day and listen to your compliments," she replied thinking how wretched she looked. Absolutely wizened.

"Are you a gardener?"

"Why yes. I'm out in the spring, summer and fall. In the winter I keep busy in the green house. Would you like to take a peek?"

"A green house. How wonderful. My biggest venture in winter is the cold frame."

"It's right off the kitchen."

Margaret followed her out of the living room with its smoky fire place through a dining room that was dominated by a large country cupboard filled with china plates, tea sets, and lidded soup and vegetable tureens to a slate floor beneath a white tile kitchen.

"Love your plank floors."

"They are original to the house. This was grandma's summer cottage. I inherited it about five years ago. The kids really have helped me out. Financially that is."

"You mean in buying out the other heirs."

"Just one other...."

"Constance?"

"Yes. She shared the same great grandmother."

"Oh dear."

"We had a devil of a time with her."

"How is Constance?" Margaret speculated that they had to pay Constance plenty for her share of the estate. Constance must have represented the interest of all of the sisters or at least presented herself as such.

"She calls occasionally to ask for money for the alumni association. I'm surprised that you've gotten involved."

"I still get the alumni newsletter," Margaret was noncommittal. She had forgotten to ask Edna just exactly what she had said to Eustacia.

Since Eustacia did not speak again of the alumni association, Margaret reciprocated and did not speak again of Constance.

"What a delight. And right off of your kitchen."

"This greenhouse was a gift from Kyle, the eldest boy. He and his friends spent all summer building the greenhouse. They decided to attach it onto the house."

"It brings light into your kitchen. In fact it lights up with whole back part of your cottage."

"I had a large window put in over the kitchen sink. Brings in a wonderful natural light doesn't it. I can look out even on cloudy days to see how the various plants are coming along. We added a heater so this winter I've been able to grow tomatoes, lettuce and spinach," she automatically picked up garden gloves, put them on and proceeded to pick tomatoes and cut lettuce. She put them into a round basket made of grapevines.

The slate floor extended out into the green house. It differed from the kitchen's only in the angle of the tilt of the floor and in the number of drains.

"Did you know that I'm on the western shore?"

"Where?"

"Just above South Neck."

"Near Maxim's place?"

"Yeah. Did you know that he has disappeared?"

"The children never tell me anything."

"Edna is helping out his partner get that business out of trouble. I'll think of that man's name in a minute. You know him. It's all financial. Anyway," Margaret sighed, "she and that awful clerk of hers are filing stuff with the court house."

"Edna?"

"Yeah. Edna the lawyer," Margaret chewed her cheek.

"Little Edna is a lawyer," she paused. "My. My. Wasn't she in Brownies with Mary Pat?"

"Was she? Ha. That's a kick. No wonder I've got so many gimp bracelets."

"Come and stay for dinner won't you? You have a long ride back. How about a simple steak, okra gumbo, and a whipped baked potato."

"Good. It'll be ready in 45 minutes," she said despite no response from Margaret.

"Eustacia. Edna is worried. And I am too. I think Maxim had gotten in some kind of trouble."

"He was always in trouble from law school on. He always came out of whatever it was smelling like a rose."

"Not this time."

Eustacia returned to the kitchen. Margaret lingered only long enough to look out over the frozen lawn that sloped down to a tilled garden lot the size of a hockey field. Beyond it yellowed pasture lands reached variously to a widening in the river.

"I don't want to alarm you."

"You know. I think Kyle might know something. He's been acting strangely lately. He has handled Max's business affairs for years. Ever since …."

"He should definitely get in touch with Dan MacIntosh."

"Max's old partner. Another name I haven't heard in years."

"Dan is a long time acquaintance of Edna's."

"Isn't it a small world we live in. Well," Eustacia sighed, "if worst comes to worst and Maxim is declared dead, his heirs should make some kind of an appearance."

They were silent for a moment.

"And is there anything to claim? Oh yeah his debts and too many wives."

"Why do you say that? Maxim was very successful."

"Margaret. He lived on the edge. He took one chance too many. Wonder what happened this time," she stood on a chair to get out a bottle of Worcestershire sauce from the top shelf of a glass front cabinet. "Not to change the subject," she climbed down. "But do you know the story about Dan MacIntosh – the partner?"

"No. Just that he worked on a subcommittee up on the Hill."

"You can bet the proverbial farm on that one. His subcommittee was under one of the finance oversight committees. They were charged with looking into the commissions set up during Reconstruction."

"What?"

"Not Reconstruction. I mean. I mean the New Deal. I think they hired some economist from one of the institutes to prepare a study who went about finding them -- the commissions not the subcommittee -- outmoded; had lived long past their functionality; were top heavy with political appointees from past administrations. Among other gruesome things."

"And the employee perks are very good. What happened," Margaret interrupted.

"The first thing that happened will not surprise you. Ironically the subcommittee was abolished and then was reestablished. Most of the commissions are still around."

"Of course. How infamous."

"Wait. Wasn't there a Hoover Commission?" Margaret decided to turn the casserole dish around in the oven. She used kitchen towels instead of an oven mitt.

"A commission to study commissions? Probably. Hoover you say."

"Yeah. Created back in the 50's."

"Those studies never really go away do they. Dan being young and innocent was devastated by the experience. He really could have gotten a job on another subcommittee. Of course, he would have had to go back to junior status. It was about that time that Max created the partnership. I don't know how or why Max decided to go into partnership with him in that little business."

"Did you finance it?"

"Most likely. At least initially. Max had an interesting way of raising funds for his ventures."

Margaret did not respond or ask a question.

"Like borrowing against his partnership interest or using my trust as collateral."

"Then he might have gotten in over his head this last time. I mean financially."

"Don't kid yourself. I think this last venture whatever it was just overcame him. He must have really gone into debt. You know looking back it seemed that every time he went into a scheme he got in over his head. We really lived from hand to mouth the whole time we were married. Really. It has just been in the last five years that I've been able to live comfortably."

"I hate to dredge up old memories."

A loud ruckus came from the drive. It was a combination of sounds - a dog barking and - the loud din of cackling from a flock of large birds.

"Chester," she looked down at her watch.

"What?"

"He's out in the truck. I'll be right back."

"Bring him in."

Margaret grabbed her coat from the mirrored Victorian hall stand. She raced down the brick path to the truck parked beyond the boxwoods.

"Chester. " He jumped out of the truck and headed straight for the boxwoods startling the flock of Guinea keats that wandered up and down the drive from the road.

"Come on." He followed her back into the cottage after some minutes of limping around the hedges and mowing back and forth along the gravel drive.

"What is it boy? Come on," Margaret asked after she let him into the hall.

He sat thumping his tail, then yawned, got up, and limped to the kitchen. Margaret brought in his dishes, filled them, and apologized for Chester's condition.

"He certainly looks peaky," Eustacia agreed.

A wind had come up from the river. The kitchen windows rattled. Chester drank water, ate his supper and crawled under the kitchen table to growl on those occasions when wind bursts moving in circular patterns across the meadows buffeted against the windows that lay in their path. He began whining. A low growling sound came out of the hall.

"Chester. Talk to me. What is it?"

"Margaret. It's just the cat. He's coming downstairs for his dinner. Henry where are you?"

A large black and tan cat with a misshapen head appeared in the doorway. Chester became silent. He rested his head on his collar. His nose twitched. The cat continued to growl.

"Now Henry," Eustacia put cat food in his dish and put it out in the pantry. "He's a good mouser."

"What happened to his head?"

"We found him out in the lower field. He could have been run over by a tractor. The kids claim his mother must have been frightened by a skunk."

With that the cat ceased growling. After he finished his meal, he walked over to Chester. Chester did not move or make a sound during Henry's close examination. On occasion his eyebrows twitched back and forth.

"Henry go upstairs. Go. I hear something in the attic. Go on."

Henry growled and hissed at Chester before turning to prance out of the kitchen.

"I must say. That is the ugliest cat I've ever seen," Margaret said candidly. She took the plates filled with steak and stuffed spaghetti squash to the dining room table. She followed without the salads.

"He's an excellent mouser and is as good as a watch dog. It's more than just a defense. At night he sits at the top of the stair."

"Are you going to get a dog," Margaret interrupted as she sat down.

She did not answer for a long minute. She took a great deal of time to speak as if she were concentrating on the table setting. She moved the glass vase filled with red carnations from the center of the table and put it on the sideboard.

"What do you think?" she emphasized the "you" not the "what."

"I think you need a watch dog out here in the country even with your Guinea keats and Henry. Besides the Guinea keats were off in the field somewhere and Henry was upstairs when I drove up to the house. I think they are easily distracted at least during daylight. A dog is focused. He or she understands guarding a territory."

"You may be right. But you must admit Henry is ferocious."

They ate in silence.

"So you want me to find out what has happened to Max."

"Any info would certainly help us. But it is really more than we expected," Margaret tore off a piece of bread filled with green olives and buttered it.

"I'm just the old info gal," she smiled. "I'm doing this for the sake of the children more than for my own curiosity," she carefully touched each corner of her mouth with a linen napkin of gingham plaid before getting up to go out into the kitchen. Margaret could hear her prepare coffee to turn on the automatic coffee maker.

Margaret picked up her wine glass to sip the last of her gift to Eustacia, Prince Michael Chablis. She noticed the gingham table cloth thrown cattycornered over the table. In the center of the table she placed a single silver candelabra. Four of its candles were lit giving off the only light in the room.

"Dan and Max had a falling out some time back. I think it had to do with something financial. Dan is smarter than he appears. My oldest

Kyle mentioned one time -- this must have happened a good three years ago -- that an investigator of some sort came around asking financial type questions about Max. Somehow Kyle thought it was Dan who sent him," Eustacia talked as she cleared the table of dishes.

Margaret made a move to get up.

"No. Sit right there. I think Kyle suspected Dan from the conversations he had with the investigator. Just what he told Kyle is another matter."

"I wonder what that was all about?"

"One of Max's wild schemes you can be sure. Dan must have been concerned about the situation. Whatever it was."

"It probably never really went away. Did you know any of the boating crowd?"

"What? His boat you mean. That was after my time. The kids might know something. They used to go out with him on weekends."

"I'm really not much help. I'll write down Kyle's phone number before I forget," she got up, went out into the hallway, and came back with a sheet of pale gray note paper with her name and address engraved above the hand written name and phone number.

It was during this time when the two women sat eating slices of apple cinnamon crumb pie and drinking coffee while cold yellow sunset faded temporarily into twilight the color of a shade of dusky rose that they decided not to speak of Max again.

"My life is hectic. I'm mayor of the village up county."

"How did you swing that?"

"I was the only local that wanted it. The incumbent was a real estate speculator. He had already annexed that acreage next to old Miss Sallie Brown's cottage. He was going to build some kind of a commercial building on it. The whole town voted him out."

"How many in the village now?"

"We have eighty people in the village. Give or take two or three."

"Hasn't changed much And tell me about yourself...."

"Well, Eustacia I think I might run for the county council. I spend a lot of time up at the county administration building anyway."

"Kyle and Michael will definitely help in any way they can."

"I do need someone who is interested in being a campaign manager. What is that noise?"

Eustacia got up quickly from the table. She left the room without speaking. Margaret continued her discourse on her ideas focusing on how she planned to execute her campaign strategy. She stopped speaking when Eustacia entered the dining room dressed in a slicker, boots, and carrying a shot gun in the crook of her arm. She walked over to the buffet to open the center drawer. After rifling through the drawer, she pulled out two cartridges. She put them into her blouse pocket.

"Good heavens. What are you dressed for?"

"I've got everything under control. It's the guineas. They're terrific watch dogs."

"Listen I've got to get back. I'll walk out with you," Margaret got up from her seat and without hesitation drank the last of coffee before hastily wiping both sides of her mouth with her napkin. "I wonder why Chester hasn't made a sound."

"Won't you stay the night."

"No. I'd love to, but I've got to get back."

They found Chester standing at the front door. He didn't begin to bark until they arrived. Above them on the landing, a growling Henry paced back and forth.

Margaret gave her a hug as they walked down the brick path.

"They come up to the house in the evening," Eustacia called back to Margaret as she ran off across the front yard and onto the adjacent field. She carefully put one cartridge into the shotgun, cocked it, and shot it off into the air in the direction of the road. She fired a second shot.

Margaret got into the truck, rolled down the window on the passenger side, and began the tedious trip down the long drive. She had to get out of the truck twice to chase the guineas off the drive. At the end of the drive, she stopped the truck to roll up the window. Chester had fallen asleep. It was there she spotted a small red bear leaning on the fender of an abandoned truck parked on the side of the road. The truck was leaning at almost a seventy-five degree angle into the roadside ditch.

"Funny I don't recall seeing that truck earlier. Whoever they are they're in for a surprise when they return."

CHAPTER 10

"Kyle. Thank you for meeting me on such short notice," Margaret got up to greet the thirty year old. Relieved that he arrived as promised, she was surprised to see how old he looked. She noted his finely etched features appeared strained even above the muted colored turtle neck, even in the dimly lit cafe.

"You caught me at a good time. So you're Margaret Longleaf. Mother has talked about you over the years. Aren't you a council woman?" He shook her hand, took off his leather jacket and put it on the back of the Windsor chair. He looked a lot like Maxim when Maxim was his age she thought. From what she could remember even his mannerisms were the same as his father's. He appeared to be preoccupied and would glance periodically over her shoulder in the direction of the bar.

"No. Mayor of a small village at the south side of Sugarfoot," she took a sip of Perrier. The glass had a piece of lime floating on top of the ice.

"Ah yes. Of course," he handed her his business card. It read Kyle Barrier general contractor. She put it down on the white linen placemat placed neatly on top of a urethane coated table. Originally from a ship's salvage yard, the wood table had been sculpted to give the illusion of a sea bed.

The plastic held beneath it sea shells and sand. She moved the thick red tinted glass candle holder over the card to study it. The candle gave off the only light at their table. Cones of light were confined to each table in this part of the cafe.

"I thought I'd see if I could get to talk to you before I drove back to the western shore. I'm down on the bay just through the end of the week. It seems a lot has happened within the last couple of days. I haven't gotten much sleep," she began. "Fortunately I'm in luck," she smiled. "Sorry for my appearance. I must look frazzled."

"You look fine. It's about Dad?"

"Have you seen or talked to him lately?" She took out the lime and squeezed it into the Perrier.

"No. Not in a while," he sighed. How about dinner."

"You mother just fixed me dinner."

"She's a good cook. Dessert?"

"She fixed that too. Maybe I'll have a second dessert with coffee," she said as the waitress approached.

"We are quite fearful that something has happened to Maxim. We need your help. By we I mean my cousin Edna. Edna's law firm is representing Dan MacIntosh - your father's partner down in South Neck," she leaned toward him and spoke softly.

"Dan. Oh yeah Dan. Dad's old partner. Something just happened. Dad you say. He's missing all right. I tried to get in touch with him last week. He never returned my call. I've had a bad feeling the last couple of days."

"You may need to call Edna," Margaret wrote her phone number on a napkin. He gave her another business card. She rewrote Edna's phone number and then wrote her own numbers on the back of the card.

"How is mother?" He took the card and put it into his wallet.

"She looks great. I really didn't say anything in detail. I didn't want to alarm her."

"About what? About Dad? She's a different person now. She runs her own business. She's pretty tough," he paused for a moment. "It's that bad."

"Where does your father keep his boat?"

"Not far from your place."

"Are you sure?"

"Yeah. Why?" He pulled his sweater sleeves up to his elbows. He wore no watch or ring.

"We went into the harbor master's office a few days ago to not only check on my slip, but also to check on Maxim's. He's not listed in the logs. Maybe he's got slip rental listed under a company name."

"Highly unlikely. He did give me the title to her. I just had the title transferred to my name."

"Nice little Saber?"

"No the Fidus Mare is not a Saber. She's a Tanya cutter."

He spoke some minutes on the outfitting of the Fidus Mare.

"Who is she named for?"

"Mother. Why do you ask?"

"Just a superstition of mine. That's good. So the Fidus Mare may have good luck on her side."

The waitress served Kyle a steak dinner and Margaret a raspberry mouse dessert at the same time.

"Dad has had some problems lately," he said after pouring steak sauce on his porterhouse. "By the way. Don't look. The guy who's probably behind all of this is standing at the bar. Sir Chatswyte...."

"What?"

"He's wearing an ascot and a monocle. Josiah Chatswyte. Manipulative."

"I've got to let the dog out of the truck. I'll do that while your eating dinner. I'll be right back. Won't be but ten minutes," she put on her wire rimmed glasses.

He watched her skirt the perimeter of the restaurant. The bar was discretely hidden behind lattice work painted white. The long bar itself was mahogany trimmed with brass railing. Although a long narrow space, it appeared much larger because the back of the bar was lined with a mahogany framed mirror and the center of the wall facing the bar consisted of a mirror framed in latticework. Two bartenders moved up and down the bar filling orders and keeping tabs. The man and the woman bartenders were dressed in white long sleeved shirts and black bow ties.

Most of the men standing or seated at the bar were dressed in starched white shirts, kaki pants, and navy blue blazers. Several wore captain's hats. Only one of these individuals wore a monocle. When Margaret passed him while he preoccupied. He was in the midst of an animated conversation. She took note that he was over six feet, slightly overweight, had blond graying hair, and wore a gold wrist watch and a ring on his pinkie.

She returned some minutes later carrying a brown paper lunch bag. She again skirted the bar, stopping to take another look at Josiah Chatswyte before returning the table. When she returned to the table, she put the paper bag on her lap.

"I would have been back sooner, except Chester did not want to get out of the truck. He is recovering from a gunshot wound."

"Hunting season. Your coffee is getting cold," he continued after he noticed her frown. "Truck? You're driving a truck?"

"It's Edna's truck. A four by four. What do you know about Mr. Chatswyte?"

"Not much except for a couple of things. He's got a financial stake in Dad."

"Your father worked for him."

"He was one of Dad's clients."

"Is this guy an Australian?"

"No. A Brit."

"I thought Maxim specialized in regulatory stuff for the Hill."

"He does. That's how he met this man."

"On the hill?"

"Yep."

"If it's the same man I just heard about at the regatta committee meeting, I think we've got some problems. Isn't this Sir Chatswyte shady? By the way, does he know who you are?"

"A bit shady. I think that is an understatement. And on top of everything else, he's a registered lobbyist. I don't think he knows who I am. Dad certainly didn't keep pictures of us kids around. At least current pictures. I've never met him. But don't underestimate him. He may know my face. He does his research. I can tell he doesn't know who I am where I'm sitting at this moment. It's dark in here. He's here on business of some sort. See the other men in that group."

"Strange. Even though I was not concentrating on the group, I thought they look familiar," Margaret turned quickly. "I can't see that far. I'll have to take another look."

"You might be safe. He looks like he's three sheets to the wind," he paused then drank his beer. "I've done some research on that joker. He works on straight commission. Ten percent I'd guess. Nothing too greedy. For someone who is that high profile, he has been able to successfully remain in the background. It's almost as if he's become part of the woodwork. As for Dad working for an alien arms dealer...," his voice trailed off. He meticulously put equal parts of butter, sour cream into the baked potato and covered it with fresh chives.

"He's here to broker an agreement. Most likely between the warring factions in Govenium and Tudmania. Once he brokers an agreement, he is free to negotiate shipments of hundreds of tons of munitions into their capitals on the pretext of resupplying their food distribution centers. You can bet one of those individuals standing around that bar represent the U.S. or a republic with an oil driven economy. Another probably represents European interests."

"As for Dad working for Sir Josiah. He might have worked for him at some point. But I got the distinct impression that he considered Chatswyte a silent partner," he continued after eating all of the steak, potato and a hard roll.

"Did you recommend this place because you thought he might show?" Margaret could not resist in asking.

"I knew that he comes here on occasion. I know he parked his boat at the marina last night. It's all in the timing. Isn't it."

"A silent partner you say."

"I got the distinct impression that the stakes were pretty high. This particular venture began about five years ago. Well, maybe not that long ago. Anyway, it has heated up within the last six months."

"The old high stakes game."

"Yes. It's as old as the Hudson Bay Company," he agreed.

"How was your father doing?"

"He was in good spirits when I last saw him. But he has been in a general decline if you know what I mean. I think whatever he was in he was in over his head. Financially, he was on the edge. He was always talking about the big deal he was going to pull off that would put him back on his feet."

"Did he seem stressed?"

"Yeah, but not any more than usual. Why?"

"I found this shoe," Margaret put the brown paper bag on the edge of the table. "While you're checking on Maxim's whereabouts could you check to see if this belonged to your father?"

"Certainly looks like something he'd wear." After a long pause he said quietly, "It doesn't look good does it."

"I'm afraid not," Margaret turned away to give the young man a moment to take in the information. She turned her head to the southeast corner of the cafe for just a short moment only to spot a figure she thought looked familiar dressed in a dark wool sweater. When he turned his face in her direction, she recognized him. It was Tory. He was seated in the back of the restaurant at a table under a large oil painting of a skipjack. The painting was almost overpowered by its mahogany frame. On either side of it hung oils of buy boats sailing through spray showers of water on the bay.

Kyle excused himself and got up. Margaret returned her attention to the young man. She watched him study the group in the bar as he passed through the cafe. She deliberately did not show any recognition of Tory nor did she mention his presence to Kyle. She rationalized that whatever Tory was doing in the roadside cafe she would find out about it at a later time. She did not look again in that direction.

She noticed that he walked as far as the bar being careful to keep clusters of people between himself and the group of men with Sir Chatswyte. He did not look at the group as he passed them. She spent several minutes studying the group, who had by this time had become boisterous. As soon as Kyle returned, she initiated and executed the successful effort to leave.

"Thanks Kyle. I've got a long drive ahead of me."

"I'll walk you to the truck," he offered.

"No. No. It's just right out front," she lied. "Please call Edna as soon as you can."

"He's got a Saber," using his glass he pointed in the direction of Sir Chatswyte.

She put on her jacket and left before he could get up. She appeared to be distracted. On the floor at the entrance to the bar she spotted a business card with a gold embossed crescent at the top center with Sir Josiah's name and company name just beneath. It was a Herron Bay crest. She picked it up and put it in her pocket. Later she would put the card in her checkbook and make a few notes on the back of her checkbook cover.

Some minutes later Kyle got up after he stuffed the shoe inside of the sleeve of his jacket he had draped over the back of his chair. When he reached the mud room, he noticed a small truck pulling out of the parking lot. A thick fog had begun to roll in as fog horns began to bleat out in the neighboring channels.

* * *

"Where's Eddie?"

Margaret did not see him until after she climbed into the truck cab. He was sitting in the corner of the seat on the passenger side so that he could not easily be seen. Chester lay at his feet.

"Tory. I thought I saw you in the back of that cafe. I'm borrowing her truck. Where do you want me to take you."

"I'm going back with you," he wished aloud.

"What about the boat."

"Oh for Pete's sake," he took out a cigarette from his inside his coat and lit it with the cigarette lighter. "You can take me down to the Cape marina. Turn left. Turn left again."

It's the next right," he opened the window at his elbow about a quarter of an inch.

She drove another two miles to the marina entrance. On coming traffic lit up the cab so that when she turned to talk to him she could see his face.

"You can stop here. This is OK. I'm a little short." They were engulfed in fog.

"Of money? Will this do?" Margaret gave him six twenties she stored in her pants pocket.

"Any more," he said under his breath.

She gave him two more twenty dollar bills.

"Edna will wire you some money tomorrow."

"This is enough."

"Is there anything you want me to tell Edna?"

"Yeah. I've got a partial report ready to go. I guess you better come aboard. You can take it to her for me."

He didn't speak again for several minutes.

"Turn right. Turn right. Park it over there behind the chart house. Next to that boat hauler," he spoke with impatience.

"While I'm here. Key to the facility."

"Here use this one," he reached in his pocket of his leather jacket and pulled out a key. "Take pooch. It's on the other side of that piling. I'm parked in 25 that key will let you in," he pointed due south to the boat slips. "Just use the top lock."

To Margaret's surprise she found clean towels, unopened soap and shampoo, and a warm locker room. The overhead fluorescent lights buzzed. She washed out Chester's dishes and fed him. He lay patiently on the floor made of red terra cotta tile in front of the door in a small entry room. His head encased in a plastic cone shaped collar lay between his paws. He growled incessantly. Occasionally he would lift his head and growl through his teeth. And when the door handle moved, he stood and yipped.

"Go on out Chester," she opened the door. He went out only to go a short distance before returning to sit at the door to the locker room.

Carrying Chester's dish under her arm, Margaret put a piece of cardboard in between the door and the lock.

"I've decided to move the boat"

"What? You scared me to death," she looked over her left shoulder. A fog bank rolled in bringing with it billowing cloud mists that glistened under the artificial lights of the marina. She could not see him, but it was Tory.

"Don't argue."

"Just making a comment. What do you want me to do?"

"Move that truck. Don't turn on your lights until you're out on the road. Go out the back way. Oh yeah. Turn left. Take the road outside the marina due south. Turn right at Pope's branch. You can't miss it. It's just past the junk yard. Follow that road for a about a mile. I'll meet you at the pier with the gas pump in about sixty. Give me a head start. And watch your six o'clock."

"With this fog. Maybe I'll make it to the gate."

"Don't complain. You're about fifty feet from the back road. It's a dirt road. Throw me the key."

Margaret threw the key out in the direction of his voice. She heard it clink as it hit the macadam. She heard nothing else except the intermittent fog horn. They went back inside the locker to collect all of her things.

"Chester you're going to have to carry your dish. You bad boy."

Margaret drove the truck with the door open holding the wheel with one hand and the door handle with the other hand in order to keep the open door steady so that she could drive and look down at the ground moving beneath her while steering the truck. As soon as she successfully maneuvered the truck onto the rutted dirt road, she found clear sky. She stopped the truck and waited for the lights from Tory's boat to move past her and then picking up the outgoing tide to move swiftly out into the channel. She could not hear its engine. She glanced up to look in the rear view mirror. Unconsciously she stopped the truck put the gear shift in neutral, pulled up the break handle, got out and looked back in disbelief to find the marina behind her was still engulfed in fog. However, she did not turn on her lights until after she drove out onto route seventeen. Route seventeen had been refurbished during the past ten years at some point after it was redesigned at the insistence of the State legislature to function as a major artery. Even though it consisted of four lanes, the lanes were so narrow and the road bed so steeply pitched along the center point that it seemed like and handled like a two lane road.

There was no oncoming or approaching traffic within sight. She drove without incident to the junk yard. The road to the marina just beyond it was hidden from view even in winter. She passed it and drove some five miles beyond before turning around.

CHAPTER 11

"Is pooch sea going?"

Without his collar, Chester shook his head before mowing up and down the pier, and then he moved about in his usual fits and starts. He sniffed around the foot of the fuel pump. An antique of sorts, its chrome handle was dotted with rust spots. He trotted gingerly along the edge of the pier between the pilings opposite the French sailor. It took him a minute to adjust to the movement near the pier caused by boat slapping against the water. Its cushions gently bumped against the pilings at intervals of time determined by water movement. He loudly sniffed the creosote saturated wood, wet from the fog and disfigured from extremes in temperature in the year round weather. He yawned, squeaked and sneezed.

"He's trained if that's what you mean," Margaret climbed into the boat without asking permission. Chester followed. The pier creaked under the strain of the fast moving tide. Unseen below but darting about the pilings were cobia, speckled trout, Spanish mackerel, spot and croaker. Some were wintering over. The movement of the boat above them brought about this sudden but temporary burst of activity. Chester cautiously walked forward sniffing the deck. He jumped when he heard an unseen splash, but made no sound. He was able to rest his head for a short moment on the teak railing. He sniffed the railing before he licked the fog residue that had collected on it.

"That's what I mean," he knelt to remove the hitches from the chinked aluminum cleats. Methodically, he threw one of them to her. It slapped upon the deck. He brought the second line with him into the boat. He stowed its bitter end in one of the storage bins lining its aft deck.

"You're casting off," out of habit she picked up and coiled her line neatly in a flat concentric circle on the foredeck. She looked up to find a continuous set of clouds that made up the fog bank rolling past the mouth of the creek a mile or two below the dock.

Thinning offshoots of mist spread out like devil fingers into the trees lining the creek bank. They wrapped around knarled, blackened tree trunks set against a luminescent mist in dark nighttime. Standing parallel, those tree trunks that did not hang over the creek were barely visible unless a traveler was passing in the vicinity. Coiled in the necks of branches of tree trunks here and there were sleeping cotton mouths who, in winter, remained invisible only to those passing below. In summer they would hang over the creek like gnarled grape vines draped haphazardly in the overhanging branches.

"It's safer. Don't worry I know these waters. By the way I don't bother with flemishing."

Margaret ignored him. She found him irritating. With all of the patience she could muster, she wiped off the wet from her levis, retied her shoe laces and pulled up her white woolen socks.

"Where did you park the truck?"

"On the other side of the entrance to the parking lot. I'd say not too far from the pier. Behind a dumpster. Why?" she walked back to the cabin to face him before speaking. They were whispering.

"I guess you're all right. Just as a precaution. I'll look at her before you leave. Come below. Out of the weather," he was able to power on the small engine with a half turn of the key. The boat vibrated ever so slightly. He lit up his pipe.

Without a word, Margaret leaned into one of the thick pilings, some thirty six inches in circumference, and pushed the sailor gently away from the pier. The engine hum and its echo was barely distinguishable from other sounds on the water. Despite the current, the boat moved slowly down the poorly marked channel to the mouth of the creek.

"This is one of my favorite gunk holes," he muttered sucking on his pipe.

"A what?"

"A place that is out of the way so to speak. Where life seems to stand still, especially in summer. A place that you can take yourself to for shelter from an oncoming storm. Or even if you're in the storm, you can easily find the creek. You know. The minute I come up into the creek. This one in particular. Everything become still. I've been in some pretty bad storms that past year. Yes, this place has a stillness about it all right. Out of the traffic."

"It's out of the traffic all right."

After maneuvering her out of the mouth and around an island generally not found on any map, he drove her about ten miles due north of the mouth of the creek before anchoring. When he went below deck, he found both Margaret and Chester asleep in a forward bunk. He went about making coffee, sorting his papers, straightening up the cabin before he could bring himself to write up his findings in a formal report. His reports were usually organized around date and time stamps, not activity. His reports were always hand written on yellow lined note paper. He sat down, adjusted the battery driven lamp, and began to write.

He awoke to find Chester sitting at his feet. He was whining. Chester had a habit of whining in a hoarse voice.

"What is it boy?" He reached over to pet the lab.

Chester jumped away. The tiny brass ship's clock fastened on the bulk head with brass screws chimed eight bells. The boat was resting in an almost motionless state as if in the dead calm. The incoming tide had not yet started its pull.

Tory opened the hatch. They climbed up onto the deck. The smell of gun powder was almost overwhelming. He choked and spit over the side.

"Go get the lady boy. Go get her," he whispered as he pulled up the anchor by hand. He started the motor and carefully steered her heading out to the shipping channel.

"I've got a rifle under the port bunk. I keep the shells in the desk drawer. Go get them," he whispered.

"Why?"

"We've got some problems."

"Have you got a windbreaker?"

"Yeah. It's stowed away somewhere. Try looking under the forward bunk. Hurry. Will ya."

Margaret returned wearing a navy blue windbreaker and binoculars. She unzipped the hood and pulled it over her head while she listened to his instructions. She sat momentarily on the forward deck to secure the rifle carefully by placing it in a teak holder before searching her pockets for her glasses. The wet from the deck soaked through her jeans. She quickly moved about to return to the cabin below. Chester followed her. She coaxed him into the bunk then retrieved her glasses from her purse, picked up a cushion, and returned to secure it before sitting on it cross legged. She sat at the bow. She released the locks holding the rifle and placed it carefully across her lap. Even in the darkness, she looked like an iridescent hood ornament.

The boat moved almost silently through the calm. Spots of open night air blew into their faces. However, as they moved up the bay the air became increasingly foul. Margaret coughed. Tory hushed her. After that she coughed into her jacket. It became difficult for them to breath.

Once they reached the fog wall and sailed through it to the other side, they found the marina outstretched before them. Popping sounds could be heard from the open bay due west. The marina lights were too dim to enable them to distinguish which slips berthed which boats. Above them the speckled dome of the milky way was barely visible even through the binoculars.

They headed out to the open bay, but keeping within the fringe edge of the fog. The opposite shoreline was not visible. This choking fog extended as far as the western shore. They motored out as far as the shipping channel before she noticed the distant lights as they tailed from the stern of a container ship heading to the port of Baltimore. The water below them shimmered like rolls of black silk. Tory brought the boat about carefully maneuvering her in order to keep her in place. They waited in the darkness.

Margaret awoke from an unexpected doze to the sound of a thud, then another and another. She opened her eyes to see a yacht anchored off the shore line just north of the marina explode in a series of bursts. Fires broke out fore and aft. Tory opened up the engine full speed and called in a may day to the coast guard. He was careful to follow along the fog wall.

"Looks like Haiphong in seventy two."

Despite the words being softly spoken, Margaret heard them. They came up behind her ears with the wind. She said nothing. She became afraid. He sounded strange, not matter-of-fact. The cold wet fog made her shiver.

He suddenly steered deeper into the fog and slowed down the engine to idle. They had come to a full stop drifting ever so slightly with the tide. The sound of another set of engines due east of them powered up then powered down.

"Come back here and bring that rifle," he said in a hoarse whisper.

She was able to walk on the fore deck along the railing and keep her balance despite the slippery surface. The water was at calm. He directed her to kneel in the cockpit. Relieved she found the deck dry.

"Stick the butt of your rifle over the bulkhead. Under the railing. There now you've got support."

Some moments passed. Then without warning a large yacht loomed between them and shore. Its great ivory bulk suddenly emerged from the dense thickly layered atmosphere. It appeared to burst through a hole in the swirling mists. Margaret jumped. Fog clung to it like a shroud. It slid through the water almost silently. It did not sound its horn. It appeared to be heading out to the open sea.

"Aim that rifle high. Up at the deck."

One man stood at the railing a good ten feet above them. The cockpit must have been another six feet above him hidden the fog. Margaret pulled out the rifle from between the bulkhead and railing, hoisted it to the crook of her shoulder and followed the figure with the rifle scope as the yacht motored past. He was barely visible. Dressed in white pants and white turtle neck sweater, his figure appeared to be partially wrapped in the light coming from a lantern attached to the bulkhead behind him. Since no light shown upon is face, he looked faceless.

This ship to their amazement was the size of a destroyer. The yacht was so large that it took a good ten minutes to complete its pass even in the limited visibility of the thick fog. It contained such a powerful set of engines that it created a wake over three feet high. She moved quickly to a sitting position in order to brace herself. The yacht moved past quickly enough, but in actuality the time it took to complete the pass moved slowly to the observer. Perhaps this massive bulk in the shrouded stillness brought about a superficial lull to the senses. Movement through the water was rhythmical. The wake it created took some ten minutes to calm. The man on the deck never looked down or acknowledged them.

"Did he see us."

"He saw us all right. They didn't want any noise."

"How long have they been out there?"

"All evening I'd say."

"Was it my imagination or was he brandishing pistols."

"I saw 'em."

"What do we do now?"

"We're going to have to zig zag around until they're out of range before we can drive out in the open," he cautiously steered the skinny water sailor due east in a random zigzag pattern keeping within the fog cover, but on course heading toward the marina.

"We're going to have to take a chance in open water. No has come out to rescue. We're going to have to do it. Lay down on the deck."

He continued calling a may day into the radio microphone every ten minutes. Margaret heard a flurry of sounds overhead. The first set sounded like a shower of hailstones. The next set sounded like a series of pings. Tory became silent. The boat shuddered ever so slightly. Then the boat began to bounce on the rapid succession of incoming chop. She looked up to see him slumped over the wheel. She sat up and fired off eight shots in rapid succession. Despite the bounce, she carefully loaded after each shot aiming high, but only in the direction of the southbound yacht. It had long since disappeared into the fog. She called Chester.

"Chester go get me the flares. Go on. Go get them," She pointed to the handle of a flair gun stored in a kit stowed in an open storage compartment. Chester lumbered past her. He sniffed around the storage compartment. He managed to move the flair gun to the deck by pulling at the line attached.

"That's it boy. Hand me the cartridges," she pulled Tory away from the wheel.

She fastened the line to the wheel. Then went below to get towels and cushions. She returned to carefully place them on the deck. She unzipped his jacket stuffed the back of his shirt with towels and managed to maneuver Tory so that he lay on his side on the cushions. He was not conscious.

She took a cartridge from a flimsy cardboard box that Chester pulled out onto the deck, loaded a cartridge and fired it. She went back to steering the boat. Chester went forward to sit at the bow. Behind them it began to sleet. Ice pellets hit the water surface.

She turned her head in the direction of the noise to find the blue heron lowering himself down out of the trailing mist as if to roost on the after deck. With great agility, he grabbed onto the railing and balanced himself. His wings outstretched momentarily closing then opening again like a fan. His wondrous sleek white head shot forward sending his feather plumes jutting upward. The moon came out to shine upon his dripping feathers. He shown in that light like a shard of ice crystal. He tucked his beak under a wing and balanced himself with one leg.

He appeared to be asleep. Within moments, the sleet stopped. The air became warm and free of the choking gun powder smell.

"Are you going to take the conn?" She asked him. A tail of moonlight trailed behind him out onto the water.

Relieved to find calm water, she set the course, tied the wheel with the line and went below again to get more towels and some blankets.

When at last she arrived at the marina, she found all that was left of the yacht, with the exception of its mast, were pieces of deck. It was fully submerged. Fire spikes were still igniting and burning in pools of oil. Debris of all shapes and sizes was thickly strewn and floating on the water's surface. Someone was out in a motor boat using flashlights to methodically search the debris. She was able to maneuver around the wreckage, dock the boat, and get help without further incident. She did not remember the heron until some time later.

CHAPTER 12

On an impulse, Margaret got up to pick up a copy of the morning Post from the top of the buffet. She stopped to admire the coconut and mocha frosted cakes set on milk glass pedestals, lemon meringue, apple and cherry pies. The deserts were displayed under glass covers in front of the mirror on various levels of the Victorian sideboard. It was then she noticed the two men. The reflection of their faces was distorted by the concave mirror. Out of habit she put on her glasses to study them taking their seats at a table placed on an angle near the southeast wall. She immediately recognized them from the breakfast earlier in the week. She recognized the two from their expensive worsted wool and suede jackets and their habit of talking loudly.

"Good morning," the waitress said matter-of-factly.

"I can tell you George is not in the least interested in proposition one eighty four. Miss Oh Miss. Alma could you bring us some cream? I hate black coffee. Are you going to take him to the airport? Can you fill me in?"

Alma left before Margaret could order.

"Sure. Sure. He is going to be sent out to RISMAR Headquarters to manage the project at least until the whole situation calms down. He went to see the doctor about his kidney stones yesterday. He's decided to replace Guy. Guy was sent down."

He paused for a moment. "I didn't think George wanted to take that tour did you?"

"Nah. The old poison tour. But someone has got to step in until a new director is selected. By the by." He lowered his voice, "George came back for reasons other than his kidney stones. I recommended he meet us for breakfast. There has been a problem of some sort with the contractor from London."

"For a RISMAR director, he was relieved pretty quick. I hate black coffee. Where is the waitress?"

"What does that tell you. He can kiss his career goodbye. He was probably out there too long. There is a reason why it's a hazardous pay tour."

"Here she comes," the dark haired man dressed in a dark suede sports jacket and tie spoke loudly. Alma ignored him.

"Well, Harry that's a matter of opinion. Oops here comes George and Lucien."

Margaret turned to get a glimpse of him stand and put a tight lipped smile on his face. He shook hands with a tall wiry man and a man who looked familiar.

"Good morning."

"Guy was questioning why the support for each the systems is handled separately. He thought that because Finsoft was already processing data at RISMAR over the wide area network with central staff messaging the data anyway, he could centralize the processing."

"I guess you know that somehow Finsoft was mismanaged?"

"Financial software George," the man who spoke to George turned to Alma as she walked by and smiled.

"Can I take your order ma'am?"

"Number two. Please. Thanks."

"The satellite support centers were and will be configured the same. We no longer have to worry about the Herron Bay takeover."

"George, don't get me wrong, we are concerned with saving money. Are you going to consolidate these sites?"

"I think that is in the future?"

After a pause, "What about wear and tear on the equipment?"

"George, equipment upgrades will begin next quarter and maintenance contracts will be in place."

"What happened? With the takeover bid?"

"Guy never showed up. It's over for now. I've got a noon flight."

"Can we take you to the airport."

"That's why I'm here."

For a moment the noise level from the watermen in the restaurant rose to a competitive pitch drowning out the end of their conversation. The number of simultaneous conversations grew until no single one was distinguishable from the others.

"Excuse me Mrs. Longleaf. Do you mind?"

"Hello yourself Sheriff McNearny."

After a thoughtful minute she put down the paper on the place setting next to hers. "I've got to go back. I closed up the house and packed the Ford. I am on my way home," she reached into her purse to pull out her glasses case. It was on the table to her left. She reached over to take out the glasses to put them on to look at the men behind him.

"What?" He sat down at the table. Her glasses were askew. He took them off and put them on the table.

"Everyone is looking."

"Watermen don't care about anything, but the day's catch," he sighed.

"I'll be back in late spring. The regatta remember. Ouch," she placed the newspaper beside her place mat.

"What did you do to your arm," he sat down opposite her facing the restaurant. He was now demanding her full attention.

"A hair line crack. Doctor says a soft cast will do."

"What about the house?"

"Keep an eye on it will you. It's Aunt Maree's house. She's a cousin on the other side of the family," she handed him a key that she had carefully placed next to her knife and spoon.

"How many cousins are in your family?" he put the key in his shirt pocket.

"Take my word for it. Lots. Did you hear? They found a body in the wreckage off St. Edmund's Hall marina," she whispered.

"What do you think?"

"I think the wreck is what's left of the Saber 28. And the body. I think it's what's left of Maxim."

"I'm sorry I wasn't much help."

The strips of plastic hanging from the door between the bar and the restaurant blew open as a man dressed in levis overalls, and a plaid shirt entered the cafe. Patches of light seemed to move in a circular motion across the ceiling. For the most part, the wavering lights were from the glare of the morning sunlight mirrored off the surface of the fast running creek. The slap and pull of high tide against the bulkhead jostled the room ever so slightly.

Margaret had deliberately picked one of the Formica tables in the northeast corner of the room so that she could talk to look out over the creek running north to south or to secretly admire the huge Victorian pine sideboard on the west wall. If she could position herself, she could admire both at the same time. However, today she noticed her favorite piece of furniture was overpowered by another massive piece filed with china and flatware. This one was topped with an even more ornate hutch lining the wall to the bar. Each was backed with a mirror. She chose to look out over the creek.

Alma returned with coffee, pancakes and bacon on her tray. She placed the meal one plate at a time in front of Margaret. She went about rearranging the jelly and sugar and setting another place.

Margaret began eating. She looked up from her plate to find Sheriff McNearny drinking his coffee and studying her. She put a piece of bacon in her mouth. She carefully buttered her pancakes and cut the stack in half. She poured syrup on her pancakes. She chewed, swallowed, then drank her coffee. She ate her breakfast leisurely.

"I'm thinking about running for the State house."

"Where does that leave us?" he picked up her hand and kissed her fingers.

"If I'm to spend time at the State house, I'll be living down here at least when the assembly is in session. She again picked up her glasses, put them on, and briefly scanned the cafe over his shoulder.

"What are you staring at. You look like you've seen a ghost."

"I think those men, at least one of them. The one that came in a couple of minutes ago. Was the one I saw in St. Edmund's Hall. And the other on the N107. Maybe not. I'm sorry. What did you say?"

Margaret reopened the paper to the business section. She did this to distract herself from an overwhelming fear. She took a series of deep breaths in an attempt to calm herself.

For the moment, Alma was the main distraction. She fussed around Margaret's table resetting a place for the Sheriff opposite Margaret. She dashed out of the kitchen with a plate of eggs and ham.

When Alma returned, she found the sheriff carefully positioned a chair to sit next to Margaret. He pulled the meal in front of him. After he finished, he took out his notebook and began writing a list. He turned his chair to face her and spoke to her for some minutes.

"Hey. Those men were in here the other day," he paused.

"Come back with me for just a little while."

"Thanks, but I've got to see Mr. Z. He promised to put on a new lock on the garage."

"OK. I'll follow you to the interstate," he promised.

The restaurant was silent as if listening for an answer.

Margaret turned to him and smiled.

The silence was broken by Alma who pushed open the kitchen door to reappear with more toast, coffee and juice and the order for two of the men behind and to the side of Margaret - one order of creamed chip beef and one of pancakes, scrapple and grits. She came back to the table several times. But each time Alma returned, she brought only a single item.

The three men dressed in worsted wool and suede jackets took advantage of Alma's hovering near Margaret's table. They continued their conversation while plying her with questions about the weather and road conditions. She grew impatient and returned to the kitchen. They eventually paid the bill and left. George, the last one to leave the cafe, threw a business card in the glass gold fish bowl.

"Never mind. Don't get up. I'll be right back," she picked up the Metro section of the paper and followed the men out into the bar. She stood at the entrance to Irma's. She wrote down their license plate numbers on the edge of the paper.

She handed Jim the paper.

"Its easy for me to run a check on them. I'll get the license plate numbers," he whispered.

"Most likely rentals," she sighed.

The group of heavily clothed watermen, who chose to sit at Formica tables neatly lining the south end of the restaurant built over one of the piers lining swift running creek, made no move to leave despite the late hour. They ate breakfast leisurely and talked continuously of the weather. On this morning only one of the watermen smoked blowing a series of smoke rings up to the ceiling where they rested as if stuck.

And out and down the creek's end the sights and sounds glistening under the morning sun, the expanse of the Chesapeake Bay stretched. Flocks of Canada geese and arctic duck were replaced temporarily by seabirds and mallards. They blanketed the surface of the water to rest intermittently only to float back down the Bay. Winter traffic on the Bay was light. No skipjacks were in sight. Only a few hunting rafts camouflaged with evergreens scurried about chasing the floating water fowl. The rafts moved across the water's surface like beetles on a pond.